TORPEDO RUN

ADMIRALTY ISLANDS

BISMARCK
ARCHIPELAGO

NEW
IRELAND

Rabaul

KarKar

Vadang Is.
Madang
Long Is.

Siassi stn

Umboi
SagSag

NEW BRITAIN

Dampier Str.

NEW
GUINEA

SOLOMON SEA

Morobe

Port Moresby

Milne Bay

N

CORAL SEA

0 10 20 40 60 80 100   150   200

TORPEDO RUN:

Mutiny and Adventure Aboard
a Navy PT Boat during World War II

by Robb White

Doubleday & Company, Inc.
Garden City
New York

For
My son, *Robb*
Torpedoman, U. S. Navy

BOOKS BY ROBB WHITE

For Young People

Candy
Deep Danger
Flight Deck
The Haunted Hound
The Lion's Paw
Midshipman Lee
Midshipman Lee of the Naval Academy
The Nub
Sail Away
Sailor in the Sun
Secret Sea
The Smuggler's Sloop
Three Against the Sea
Torpedo Run
Up Periscope

Non-fiction

In Privateer's Bay
Our Virgin Island

Novel

Run Masked

CONTENTS

BOOK ONE
The Boat 1

BOOK TWO
The Sea 105

B O O K O N E

The Boat

She was
nameless, with only a number given to her by the Navy, but
her crew called her *Slewfoot.* She was 77 feet long, 20 feet
wide and drew 4 feet of water. When her temperamental
engines were right and her bottom was clean she could go
60 miles an hour, which, for a boat, is *very* fast. In the
narrow waters around Bayonne, New Jersey, where she was
built, she looked pretty big. On the vastness of the Pacific
Ocean, going about her deadly business in the dark nights of
war, she was a splinter.

During World War II, *Slewfoot* and the rest of the PT
boats were the smallest warships the Navy had. Like many
small things in Nature, *Slewfoot's* life depended on her speed,
for she had no protection against gunfire, torpedoes, bombs
or strafing planes. Unlike the Navy's other ships, she had no
armor; there was nothing for a man to hide behind when the
tracers began to arc toward him, for *Slewfoot* was built of
wood and mostly plywood at that.

She was designed to hit and—run. Designed to carry three
engines with the combined ram of four thousand horsepower
to get *Slewfoot* into position and—out again.

Seventy-seven feet of plywood carrying a wallop. On the
forepeak there was a 37-millimeter cannon. On both bows
were 20-millimeter cannon. Amidships forward were two
rocket-launching racks. A little aft of them were two sets of
twin .30-caliber machine guns. Farther aft, two on each side,

were twin .50-caliber machine guns in turrets. On the stern there was a Bofors 40-millimeter cannon. Sometimes there were more guns than there were men to shoot them.

In addition to the guns, cannons and rockets, *Slewfoot* carried two flip-over torpedo racks each armed with two torpedoes capable of sinking any ship afloat.

And, against submarines, she had depth charges in racks on the stern.

Riding *Slewfoot* in battle was a little like riding a bomb. In her tanks she carried three thousand gallons of highly explosive aviation gasoline. When the PTs were hit they rarely sank in the slow and heartrending way of other ships. PTs simply vanished in one quick, awful flash of flame and smoke.

Compared with other warships, *Slewfoot* was manned by a bunch of kids. The oldest man aboard was the Captain, an ancient twenty-one. The rest of them were nineteen, eighteen, even seventeen years old. There were usually a dozen men riding *Slewfoot* through the dark sea, their eyes straining for sight of the enemy, engines muffled, guns manned and ready.

There were motor machinist's mates—"motormacs"—to baby the three Packard engines; torpedomen for the "fish"; gunners. There was a quartermaster who watched over the charts and the movements of the ship; and a boatswain's mate—the bosun—to care for the boat itself. There was a radarman to watch the thin line going around and around; and, of course, the cook. There were two officers—the captain and the executive officer.

The men could sleep in the "dayroom" forward, just abaft the chain locker, in bunks along the sides. It was like sleeping in a crowded elevator that had broken loose and was falling to the bottom of the shaft, over and over. But you got used to it just as you got used to standing forever with your knees loose and bent, and learned, many the hard way, what the man meant when he said, "One hand for you and one hand for the ship."

It took you only once to find out why they told you not to fall down on a PT boat. Standing up, holding on, your bent, loose knees absorbed the pounding of the hull against the sea, your body balanced with the astounding roll and pitch. If you fell down, when you tried to push yourself up, the deck dropped out from under you, then the boat came up as you came down. It was like trying to stand up on the bare back of the father of the Strawberry Roan.

One hand for you, one hand for *Slewfoot*.

The PT boats would take on anything—if the skipper and the crew had guts enough. The size of the enemy's battle-ships was awful, but the PTs took them on in wholesale lots. They fought it out with destroyers, cruisers, carriers, barges, landing craft, aircraft, even submarines and artillery on the shore. They lost some, they won some.

A battleship can stand off twenty-five miles away and paste you. PTs can't do that. They've got to go in close and hit and get out—if they can. The boats can do it—all it takes is a skipper with guts enough and a crew who believes in the skipper.

The Skipper of *Slewfoot* was a quiet, small, inoffensive man named Jones with the courage of a lion. Jones never raised his voice, never seemed angry or depressed or—afraid. If Jones said, on *Slewfoot*, "Let's go get 'em," the crew were ready to go get 'em. They had absolute faith in Jones. If he took you in close to the enemy—so close you could see the men behind the guns that were shooting at you—he'd bring you out again. Or so they said on *Slewfoot*.

In a little boat like that, where the twelve men lived so closely together—and died together—there was a feeling you didn't find on the big ships. There wasn't room for the too-bad-Jack-I'm-getting-mine attitude; no room for the selfish man, or for the coward (although every man on *Slewfoot* had been scared stiff, many times), or for the griper and the dis-content. If you didn't like duty on *Slewfoot*—out. Just like that—out. If you couldn't get along with your shipmates—

out. If you couldn't stand up in the searing blaze of the enemy's searchlights with the stuff he was throwing at you like a fiery wall and shoot—out.

And if you didn't believe in the Captain you were in trouble.

In the daytime *Slewfoot* hid up one of the stinking New Guinea rivers, covered from stem to stern with big tropical leaves and branches so the enemy airplanes couldn't spot her and blast her in the daylight. In the daytime *Slewfoot's* crew lived on Snob Hill back in the jungle but not out of sight of their boat.

Snob Hill was a charming place to live. When it wasn't raining it was getting ready to rain in five minutes. The number of bugs that could bite you, sting you, eat their way into you, walk on you and spit in your eye was unbelievable. There couldn't be that many bugs—but there were.

Snob Hill was an area of mud a little higher than the rest of the mud. The regulation two-foot tent pegs were useless; the crew of *Slewfoot* used pegs ten feet long and even they didn't get to the bottom of the mud.

The tents were a dirty, greenish gray and looked about like the jungle all around them. To keep their cots from sinking out of sight into the mud while they slept, the men strapped tree limbs to the cot legs. You started out with the cot up against the ceiling of the tent—you woke up level with the mud, sometimes below it.

All manner of things lived in the mud—frogs, lizards, salamanders, snakes, worms—but the worst were the leeches. They were long, slimy, and black. All you had to do was put your foot down in the mud and the leeches would appear, squirming toward you—so many of them that it looked as if the mud were moving. If you couldn't get out of the mud and tear them off, they could suck you dry.

One day in 1943, the crew of *Slewfoot* was down on the strip of mangy beach between the jungle and the sea trying to dig a hole in the soggy ground. It was raining and the rain soaked the ground they were digging in and poured into their hole faster than they could scoop it out.

Finally the Executive Officer, whose name was Peter Brent, stopped digging for a moment, looked up at the gray, close, soaking clouds and said, "This is no place for him. Let's get the boat and do it right."

The crew, soaked with rain and covered with mud, stopped digging and looked at him, surprised. A PT has no business on the open sea in daylight, for then she can be seen and an enemy ship can stand off out of her range and slaughter her. Or the planes, like vultures in the sky, can swoop down on her and take her.

The Executive Officer knew that just as well as the crew did but maybe he was a little closer to it. Anyway, he walked away from the hole full of mud and rain, and the rest of the men, carrying their shovels, followed him back through the dripping, foul-smelling jungle to *Slewfoot*.

The chief motormac's name was Sko. In the records of the Navy it was written Skowalskilatovich or something like that, but on *Slewfoot* his name was Sko. Next to Jones, the Skipper, Sko was the oldest man aboard—twenty—and had more time in the Navy even than the Skipper and the Exec. And he was a good motormac who could nurse those three big Packard engines into life when nobody else could make them do anything but shine. Now he dried off the ignition harnesses while the rest of the crew got ready to go to sea.

They took the rotting tarps off the guns and rockets and torpedoes and cannon and unlimbered everything that could shoot. Sam, the cook, went up to Snob Hill, climbed the topless palm tree and took down the flag that flew there night and day. It was, Sam noticed, ragged on the free end and stained with the steam from the jungle, but it was still the flag. He folded it the way he had seen the Marines do it and carried it down to *Slewfoot*.

Then, when Sko got a roar out of the Packards, they

untied *Slewfoot* from the trees on the bank and started easing her down the river.

"We'd better muffle 'em," the Executive Officer called down to Sko. "Don't want to wake up any shore batteries."

Sko, who sat in a tractor seat right over the engines, put the mufflers on the exhausts so that the roar died to a low purr—and the speed dropped off. Some of the crew thought Sko had the dirtiest job on the boat. Sitting over the engines that way, he got all the heat they put out, and the sickening fumes of gas and oil and rubber. And when the Skipper shoved the three throttles forward, the sound of the engines became so great that, to Sko, it seemed solid. Those things didn't worry him as much, though, as another thing. Sko never knew what was going on topside—never knew when an enemy shell was going to come in there with him and wipe out him and the engines and the gas and the boat. He just had to sit there in the bouncing tractor seat and listen to the guns yammering up on the deck and wait.

The Executive Officer conned the boat slowly down the river, ducking his head under the low-hanging and concealing jungle. It was like going down a dark green, soaking wet tunnel, but at the far end he could see the Pacific, now gray and closed in by the rain.

This was a dangerous thing to do and the Navy wouldn't like it if they heard about it. But, he thought, it's the only decent way to do it.

The men stood at their battle stations, looking down the greenish tunnel. None of them had anything to say and none of them looked aft at the flag.

Slewfoot slid out of the jungle's shelter and as she did, the rain stopped and, suddenly, the sun shone and even the brown water seemed to sparkle.

"That helps," the Executive Officer remarked to Murphy, the quartermaster. "That's all we need—plenty of sun so the Japs can see us from here to Tokyo."

Murphy, a beat-up little Irishman who looked a lot older

then he was, didn't say anything. This was the worst day he had ever known and he was afraid that if he started talking about it he might begin to cry. He tried to figure that it was all just part of the war and that's the way it went, but it didn't do any good. He was glad when the Exec shoved the throttles forward—now he had something to do.

Slewfoot's lean, curved bow came up and her squat stern went down and she *moved*. All hands were rocked back on their heels as the boat leaped forward, throwing two perfectly formed sheets of brownish water away from her.

The Executive Officer took her out on the sea until she was clear of the great roil of dirty brown New Guinea water flowing from the mouth of the river and was in the clean, blue, shining water of the Pacific itself.

All hands were alert now as they always had to be in the PT boats. Some scanned the cloud-rimmed sky for planes, some searched ahead, some to the side, while others watched the long green line of New Guinea—watching for the little flashes of guns. There was a finger on every trigger; Sko was watching the engines, making sure that, if it was needed, they would put out everything they had; the Exec, standing on the little steering platform, half his body above the nothing windshield, wiped spray out of his face and looked ahead.

Then the Exec rang for all engines stop and pulled the throttles back. *Slewfoot* lost her balance and settled heavily in the water to lie there, wallowing in the slow waves. Now she was awkward and uncomfortable to be aboard for she was built to *go*, not to lie there thrown this way and that by the sea.

The Executive Officer said, "All hands stay at your battle stations except you, Murph, and you, Preacher."

The Preacher was a rated torpedoman named Welborn who said that if he survived the war he was going to wander all over the world preaching to the people not to fight each other any more.

The Exec and Murph and the Preacher went aft past the

40-millimeter cannon, past the depth charge racks, past the smoke generator, all the way to the stern.

The Executive Officer said, "Make it short, Preacher. It'll be like shooting fish in a barrel if we get caught out here with no way on."

The Preacher said, "I don't know how it goes—in the Book."

"Just say the way you feel," the Exec told him.

The Preacher went to stand beside the flag. "Oh Lord," he said, "please let this man be welcome in Your Kingdom for he was the best man we ever knew. Amen."

Then the Exec and Murph and the Preacher did the wrong thing, for the flag is not supposed to go too. But they left the flag wrapped around the Skipper when they rolled him off the stern, and in the water it unfurled a little as it sank, the red and white and blue growing dimmer until they couldn't see it any more.

It began to rain again as they went forward and Sko started the engines. You couldn't tell on the way back if any man aboard *Slewfoot* had tears in his eyes because their faces were wet with rain, but every one of them looked back at least once to the unmarked place in the Pacific Ocean where Jones, the Skipper, was buried with the flag.

In the days to come every one of them wished with all his heart that Jones had not been killed.

Peter Brent, the Exec, and Sko were sitting in the crew's quarters listening to the rain thudding on the deck above and talking about the war and the future of *Slewfoot* and the death of the Skipper.

After the battle for Guadalcanal, the United States forces were moving westward again, driving against the Japanese, who had moved, since 1941, down into the southwestern

Pacific islands, just as they had moved into the Philippines, Guam and all the islands of the Central Pacific. On land and on sea this was bitter, mean, dirty fighting, the terrible land and its stinking jungle almost as great an enemy as the Japanese. The mission of the PT boats was to stop the flow of reinforcements coming over the sea from the Empire, to sink the ships carrying troops and supplies before they could reach the shores of the islands.

"We got a long way to go," Sko said, looking at a map of the Pacific. He didn't do this often because it always depressed him. So far to go. The immensity of the Pacific. The miles and thousands of miles of that ocean. With, at last, the islands of the Japanese far to the north. On the land areas scattered across these miles a lot of Marines were going to die and on those millions of square miles of Pacific a lot more sailors were going to die.

Slewfoot was tied up to trees on the banks of the Morobe River, which flowed out of the island of New Guinea in the Bismarck Archipelago. Sko was sitting on a narrow wooden bench only 8° south of the Equator but 148° east of Greenwich, England. A year ago he had never heard of New Guinea, the Arafura Sea, the Morobe River.

Sko folded the map so he couldn't see it. "Man, I never thought I'd ever wind up in a place like this," he said.

"You haven't been anywhere yet," Peter Brent told him. "Wait until you hit the bright lights and soft music of Walingai, Madang, Wewak, Kairiru, Valif—or Aitape, now that's a spot."

"So what are the poor people doing today?" Sko looked over at Brent, wondering how to say what he wanted to say without being a greaseball. He just couldn't say, "Peter, next to the Skipper, you're the best PT-boat officer in the Navy and I—and all the rest of the crew—want you to be skipper now." So what could he say?

He said, "Are they going to let you stay as skipper, Mr. Brent?"

"I don't know," Brent told him.

"All they've got to do is send us out one of those shiny ensigns they've got in Melville, Rhode Island. Wouldn't take long to get the shine off him and make an executive officer out of him. Then we'd be set."

When Brent didn't say anything it worried Sko. "You *want* to be skipper, don't you? I mean, you don't want somebody else running the boat, do you?"

"How would you feel, Sko, if somebody said, 'Okay, you take Jones's place'?"

"I see what you mean. He had *big* shoes. And when I first saw him I said to myself, 'Oh, oh, we're in trouble.' Remember that day in Tulagi when he came through the mud with his pants rolled up and said he was going to be the new skipper? He looked like one more drop of rain would wash him clean away. Man, he was *wispy*. And I thought to myself, 'That little twerp can't fight his way out of a wet paper bag with a hole in it.'" Sko looked up at the overhead where the rain was soaking through the patch the bosun had put on the shell hole. "I was wrong."

"You were wrong."

"I don't go for these big, serious words," Sko said, still looking at the film of rain running along the plywood, "but Jonesy was *all* courage. And I don't mean like these guys who'll walk up and slap a giant and get their brains beat out. Jonesy would figure it out so he slapped the giant *down*." Sko kept on looking at the overhead. "What I mean is, skipper, you were right there with Jonesy all the time. You never said well maybe we ought to pass this one up, or not go in so close, or slip on by in the dark. You never did."

"With Jonesy it wouldn't have done any good," Brent told him.

"What I mean still is . . . well, I think if they let you go on running the boat we'd come out okay. The Navy ought to be able to see how logical that is. You know us and we know you and old *Slewfoot* could keep on blasting 'em like she always has. Just send us one of them shiny ensigns for an Exec."

Coming down to the boat, stomping through the rain and mud, Murphy, the Irish quartermaster, was in a wild Irish fury. They couldn't do this! The stupid, ignorant Navy sitting in their swivel chairs in Washington, D.C., couldn't do this!

He banged across the gangplank, stomping some of the mud off his feet, and stomped across the deck and went below to where Sko and Peter Brent were sitting. From inside his dripping poncho Murph took out the damp dispatch and laid it on the mess table, pressing it out flat with his hands. "There must be a mistake. They must mean some other boat," he said.

Peter Brent read the damp typing and then looked at Sko. "This answers your question, Sko. The new skipper of *Slewfoot* is a jaygee named Adrian Archer who is on his way out here now."

Sko stared at Brent, not believing him at first, but when belief began to come Sko began to feel the way he did every time just before a patrol. A sort of sick, queasy feeling in his stomach and cold spit running around his teeth.

Murphy began to yell. "Adrian! What kind of name is that? That's a girl's name! Adrian!"

They didn't pay any attention to the little Irishman. Sko said, "Where's he coming from—one of the other boats? I never heard of him, though."

Murphy was still yelling. "One of the other boats. In a pig's eye! He's coming straight out of that school in Rhode Island." Murphy slumped down on the bench. "So they send us a man with a girl's name who's never even seen this ocean, never even seen one of these stinking islands. Never had one of those Japanese searchlights bore a hole right through his eyes—followed by a bullet. They can't do this to us, Mr. Brent."

Peter said, "Calm down, Murph. This guy might be the best PT-boat skipper in the world."

Murph turned his fury on Brent, but he kept it under control and only said, very quietly, "The best PT-boat skipper in the world is lying out there in the water, dead." And then all the fury went out of him and he just sat, staring across the table. "When Jonesy got it," Murph said, "I felt like my own father had gotten it. No, I guess it wasn't like that because I never knew my father. Like it was my own brother. Of course, Jonesy was an officer and all that, but I thought a lot of him."

"We all did," Peter said. "But he's dead and the boat's getting a new skipper. Maybe he doesn't know as much about things as we do, so it'd be a good idea to help him learn—fast. Because the faster he learns the better it's going to be for all hands."

Murphy said, "I just hope he isn't one of these Stateside tigers going forth to war and not knowing his belly from a belaying pin." Then he laughed. "I don't know what a belaying pin is myself."

"It's something to hit Irishmen on the head with," Sko told him.

Murphy glared at Sko. "If you had a name I could pronounce, I'd call you something."

Brent stood up. Then, with his fingernail, he scraped the wet dispatch up off the table, folded it and put it in his pocket. "Okay, let's go yachting," he said.

Slewfoot was no yacht but there was a *little* space below decks that wasn't filled with engines, gas tanks, ammunition and running gear. Forward, in the forepeak, there was a chain locker for ground tackle, and then the dayroom with the tiered bunks for the crew. Then Sam's tiny galley where, in spite of having nothing to cook with, he could come up with some pretty tasty chow. On the port side, just under the bridge, there were two tiny staterooms—one for the captain, one for the executive officer—and between these and the cramped engine room was another small space for the crew. From there on aft it was all engines.

Peter went into the captain's cabin to get the charts of the area the boat was going into.

Jones's cabin was a lot like Jones: neat, his clothes all folded and stowed, his bunk made up and the corners squared. There were no pin-up girls on the bulkheads, only a picture of Jones's parents in a silver frame. There were a few books, mostly technical; Jones's Navy file; some personal letters; a little pile of magazines and, on the fold-down desk, Peter's own fitness report half filled out.

Jones had written in the space on the fitness report:

Ensign Peter Brent, USNR, is an outstanding officer in all respects. Courageous but not foolhardy, loyal, intelligent; a natural leader of men; an excellent seaman; a dignified and decent man of the highest integrity. He is highly qualified, and strongly recommended, for command.

Jones had not signed it, so Peter tore it up and dropped it in the little wastebasket.

When they got back from this patrol, Peter decided, he would inventory all Jones's belongings, and somehow ship them back to his parents. He would also have to write that letter telling these gentle, handsome people in the silver frame that their son was dead—killed in action against the enemy.

On deck Peter could hear the footsteps of the crew—soft in the flight-deck boots—moving around, preparing for sea, but, for a moment, he stayed in the closed cabin.

Peter had wanted command of *Slewfoot*—and had thought that the crew wanted him to have command. With the months of Jones's example of absolute bravery and beautiful boat-handling and the subtle but tremendously effective method Jones had for training the crew until they were the best in the Navy, Peter thought that he could have made a good skipper for *Slewfoot.* Not so good as Jones, but good enough.

He took out the dispatch and looked at the name Adrian Archer again. Who was he? What was he like?

And why, Peter thought bitterly, did they have to send this Adrian Archer to take over command? Why couldn't they have let him have it?

Murphy stuck his head down through the hatch and yelled, "Ready for sea, Captain."

"Coming up," Peter said. Then he tore up the dispatch and dropped it into the wastebasket with his useless fitness report.

The sun had not yet set but the rain clouds made it almost dark as *Slewfoot* slid down the muddy river on the center engine. When she reached the open sea, Sko cut in No. 2 and No. 3, Peter shoved the throttles forward until the tachometers read 1900 and *Slewfoot,* as though enjoying it personally, went up to a slam-banging 35 knots.

Peter called back to Murphy, who stood at the dimly lit table in the little chart house just abaft the bridge, and gave him a northwesterly course. Murph laid it out with the parallel rulers. The course went through the Dampier Strait between New Guinea and New Britain and then back along the coast of New Guinea.

In a moment, Murph stuck his head out of the chart house and said to Peter, "If you hold that course you're going to run right over Vadang Island."

"That's where we're going," Peter told him.

Jason, the gunner's mate, said over his shoulder, "What's to shoot there?"

"Nothing, I hope," Peter said. "The Army's thinking about using Vadang as a close-in staging area and wants to know if there're any troops to be cleared off first."

Murph was indignant. "So the Army's got eight million fine young American boys and they have to send a Navy man to see if there's any enemy around."

"Not like that," Peter told him. "I just broke the first law of the Navy."

Murph stared at him in exaggerated horror. "You didn't . . . *volunteer?*"

Peter nodded. "Well, not exactly. I heard the Army talking about it, so I said since we went past the island on most of the patrols, I'd be glad to take a look for them."

"Who's going ashore?" Murph asked.

"I am," Peter said. "And you are."

"So we have a stroll in the tropical moonlight," Murph said, "with rain running out of our ears. There's nobody on that island. We've been past it a dozen times. There aren't even any of those dusky maidens with their red teeth filed down to the gums."

Jason, the gunner, who was a very serious young man, said, "If there were any Japs on Vadang why haven't they opened up on us?" He patted his guns affectionately. "I wish they had."

"Well, we'll have a look," Peter said.

"Why don't we just anchor the boat, have a good night's sleep, and tell the Army in the morning there's nobody there?" Murph asked.

"Tell the Army a *lie?*" Jason asked. Murphy's ideas frequently shocked him.

"What's a lie?" Murphy cried. "There's no enemy on that island, so what's a lie?"

"Oh, well . . ." Jason said, and turned back to his guns.

"Find out how close we can get to it," Peter told Murphy. "I don't want to row that raft more than fifty miles."

"I'll put you so close we can step ashore, skipper," Murph said, and went back into his little house.

Peter stood on the steering platform looking from the dimly lighted compass to ahead and around and back to the compass. The crew was settling down now—at battle stations, but relaxed, some lying on the deck in any shelter from the spray, others sitting around yakking quietly. This crew was used to the long, tedious patrols—sixteen, eighteen, twenty hours at a stretch—and they took it easy when they could because, at any instant, they might be in the middle of a war.

Peter stood alone on the bridge thinking his own thoughts. Going ashore on Vadang wasn't bothering him—he and Murphy could explore the whole island in three or four hours —and if anything came along while they were ashore, the crew could take *Slewfoot* out of there and come back later.

Vadang wasn't bothering him, but this Adrian Archer was.

Slewfoot and her crew had been fighting for a long, long time and it was beginning to tell. The men weren't keeping the boat shipshape the way they once had; there was more oil in the bilges than water; there was a dank, unhealthy smell of unaired bedding in the quarters; rust was beginning to show where it should not have shown; the decks hadn't been swabbed down for weeks.

The neglect of the boat was one thing, and you could excuse it. The men of *Slewfoot* were living in misery, patrolling the dangerous sea at night from early dusk until late dawn; then they came "home" to the mud and bugs and crummy chow and silent jungle.

It was telling on them, Peter realized. There were more fistfights among them now; bitter fights over nothing at all. More griping, more talk of Stateside, more homesickness— and more real sickness: malaria; the "crud," which made any scratch, any leech bite a real wound; dysentery.

His men had, he thought, just barely enough strength left to fight when it was time to fight.

What was this Adrian Archer going to do to them? These were tired, worn-out men living on a razor's edge between sanity and the polite phrase for insanity: "combat fatigue." They had to be handled with care and treated with respect and decency—which they so truly deserved—and, above all, leniency. If Adrian Archer turned out to be one of these big, bull-necked men with a loud voice and a hard nose the crew of *Slewfoot* was going to slip off that razor-edge and it wasn't going to be on the right side. Just a little of orders being bellowed at them, just a little criticism instead of praise, and this crew in the dark around him now would fall apart. Just a little of that "black-shoe Navy" would totally demoralize and defeat the weary crew.

Peter hoped that Adrian Archer would turn out to be a kind and intelligent man, a man who would listen a little, and learn a little.

Above all, Peter hoped, let Adrian Archer have some courage. When you got down to the bottom of it, all that had held this crew together so far had been that courage of Jonesy's. If Adrian Archer had only a little of that the crew could go on fighting for a long time to come.

Peter turned in the semidarkness and looked over at the starboard corner of the bridge. Now it was empty. The chair wasn't there. Jones wasn't there.

How many times, Peter wondered, had he seen Jonesy sitting over in that corner during the long, long nights? In the early days, Jonesy had used an ammo can to sit on, but in some port some member of the crew—no one asked who— had swiped from somewhere a canvas folding chair like the ones movie directors use. From then on, as soon as it got dark and the boat was on its way and squared away, Sam, the Negro cook, would come up on deck with the Skipper's Chair and unfold it and set it up in the after starboard corner of the bridge for Jonesy to use when he didn't have the wheel.

Jonesy had not been the kind of man who went around saying that because he was the Captain, you do this and you do that. Whatever he wanted done always seemed to you to be, first, a thing that would make you feel better, or safer, or more useful and important. Then, second, it would be a thing to make *Slewfoot* more shipshape, more dangerous, more effective.

Jonesy never said, nor even by his actions gave you the idea, that this was *his* chair and for you not to sit in it. But

2

no man on *Slewfoot* would have sat in the Skipper's Chair. It wasn't, Peter thought, that they wanted to but were afraid to. They just didn't want to. It was the Skipper's Chair, and he needed it and deserved it.

It was a very nonregulation chair with the wooden, folding frame painted white and the canvas dyed blue. From somewhere else one of the crew had purloined a set of those rubber feet that fit on crutches and put them on the chair so it wouldn't slide all over the bridge.

Peter remembered the night of the name. Jonesy had been using the chair for a few weeks by then and, on this night, Peter had had the wheel and they were ghosting along the enemy shore when, from behind him, he heard the Skipper laughing out loud.

"Look what these crazy guys have done," he said to Peter.

On the canvas back of the chair someone had stenciled QUEEN MARY in white letters.

Peter, facing forward now, was startled by someone behind him touching him on the shoulder. He whirled around and it was Murph.

"You want me to steer her, skipper?" Murph asked. And then he made a movement to starboard with his head.

In the dark, Sam was unfolding the Skipper's Chair and setting it up in the corner.

Peter stepped down off the steering platform as Murph stepped up but he didn't go over to the chair, just stood looking at it as Sam finished putting it in place.

There's no reason, Peter thought, why I shouldn't sit in that chair. No reason at all. Until Adrian Archer turned up he was skipper and so should sit in the Skipper's Chair.

He went over to Sam and said, "I won't need that, Sam. We're only going up the coast a little way."

"Well, you ought to rest when you can rest," Sam told him.

Somehow the men had gathered and were watching Peter. Even Sko had come up out of the engine room.

"Thanks anyway," Peter said, "but I won't need it."

One of the men said out of the dark, "Go ahead and sit in it, Captain."

Without saying anything, Peter sat down in the chair. Around him in the dark the men stood for a moment longer and then they drifted away to their stations.

It took four hours to get to Vadang. Peter conned the boat slowly toward the dark, deserted-looking island, with the bosun standing forward with a lead line and whispering back the depths of the water. When he was in as close as he could get, Peter motioned for the anchor to be dropped and then cut the throttles.

Murph came out of the chart house looking like a one-man war. On a cartridge belt he had not one, but two big Colt .45 automatics, and every loop was filled with an ammo clip. Around his neck he had an aviator's shoulder holster with a .38 Smith & Wesson revolver and a bandolier of bullets. He was also carrying an M-1 rifle and his pockets were bulging with clips for it. In case all this failed, he had a Marine fighting knife stuck in his belt.

Peter looked at him in the dark and said, "Shoot much?"

Shadows forward came out of the hatch with the deflated rubber boat and put it down on the deck as Peter and Murph came around the bridge.

They unlashed the boat and then began pulling the CO_2 bottles, which went off with a loud hissing.

In the dark Peter waited for the gas to inflate the rubber compartments, blowing them up into the shape of a more or less rectangular boat, but as the gas bottles emptied themselves and stopped hissing, the outline of the boat did not change—it just lay on the deck, a limp rubber wad.

Then one of the men said, "Look at the hole in this thing!"

They picked the boat up then and, against the dark sky, they could see where the shell that had killed Jonesy had also gone through three folds of the boat.

"What about the patch kit?" Peter asked.

"It's not meant for holes that big," the man said. "It's just for little holes, bullet holes—not for cannon."

"Is this the only boat aboard?"

"Yes, sir. You remember, the skipper of that One Twenty boat borrowed our other one and I guess it went down with the One Twenty. They never issued us another one."

Peter looked over at the dark outline of Vadang Island. Now, with no rubber boat, it looked a lot farther away.

"Can we get in any closer, Murph?" he asked.

"Lots of coral in there," Murph said. "We might get away with it, but if we didn't it'd take the bottom out of the boat."

Peter looked at the distance again. The island was at least two miles away—a long swim in anybody's league. And he didn't particularly want to meet one of those New Guinea crocodiles in the middle of the night—they were bad enough in the daytime.

He had only told the Army he would take a look, and this was as good a look as he could take.

"Okay, let's get the anchor up and get out of here. We'll get a new boat and try it tomorrow night."

Over on Vadang nothing moved, no light showed, no smoke.

3

To stop the advance of the United States forces through the jungles of New Guinea the enemy was pouring troops, guns, ammunition, planes and supplies into its great staging area on the northeast corner of New Britain Island with the town of Rabaul as a base. No United States attacks on Rabaul had been able to stop this flowing in and, worse, flowing out of the enemy. The best we could do was to force him to move only at night. In the daytime, U. S. Navy and Air Corps planes had just enough edge on the enemy's air cover to make it dangerous for him to try to get his convoys of troops and supplies under way. But at night we could not stop him.

From all over the Japanese Empire, ships carrying the stuff of war flowed through the night into Rabaul and, at night, flowed out again, bound for New Guinea.

For us it was an all-Army show except for the little PT boats of the Navy. Their job was to stop this flow of the enemy out of Rabaul into the area of the fighting on New Guinea. It was hard and dangerous work and the kind of fighting that is most dreaded by all men.

It isn't hard to fight when you know that the enemy is in a certain place and you must go to that place and fight him. You, and your buddies, thousands and thousands of them, go there and fight.

In the PT boats you had maybe a dozen buddies in a tiny boat, in the dark. You didn't know *where* the enemy was or how strong he was or when, in the black of night, he would shoot you. You did know, though, that against the enemy's ships you had to hit him with everything the boat had to kill him, while with one shell, one lucky hit of even a light deck gun, he could wipe you out.

In armies of men, war doesn't seem very personal to any one man. He's just a tiny, invisible, unimportant part of an enormous machine. In the PT boats war is personal, bitter, hard. No PT boat ever fought an even fight; the odds were always hundreds, thousands to one against the men in the PTs. When you sighted the enemy in the darkness he was always immensely bigger and stronger than you were with more and bigger guns . . . more *everything*. To survive in PT boats took three things, all at the same time: gunnery, seamanship, guts.

So, in the dark nights, the PT boats would fan out across the sea-lanes between Rabaul, on New Britain, and New Guinea. There they would make their lonely and dangerous patrols, all night long, their radars searching out the enemy as he tried to creep past them.

On *Slewfoot* the man in the bow called back softly, "Anchor's aweigh." Peter eased the throttles ahead, swinging the boat around Vadang Island and resuming the patrol along the New Britain coast.

The PTs usually cruised as close to the land as they could, for the land was their protection. The enemy's radar signals were reflected from the great mass of the land so that the tiny, moving blip of a PT boat was hard to pick out.

The night was clear now, but very dark, the sky covered with a high layer of solid cumulus. As soon as they were clear of Vadang, Murphy took over the wheel and Peter went back to Jonesy's chair and broke out the big night binoculars.

The only light aboard *Slewfoot* now was the tiny pool of dim light around the face of the compass and, coming up through the hatch, a faint, dim, green glow from the radarscope. There was actually more light in the phosphorescence of the sea as they slid through it.

There was almost no noise. Mixing with the whine of the superchargers, well muted by Sko, was the lap lap of water against the bow. Occasionally a man would cough, or you could hear a word or two as the watch was changed.

Silence and stealth were *Slewfoot's* real weapons, plus speed.

Murph turned around and whispered over to Peter, "Moon'll be up in about an hour. Full, too."

"The better to see you with, Goldilocks," Peter said. But he hated moonlight. To him on a moonlit night *Slewfoot* seemed to stick out like a sore thumb, making a beautiful target for anyone with a gun.

As he sat there, scanning the sea ahead and to both sides and occasionally looking aft, occasionally lowering the glasses to look around what was—for this night anyway—"his" boat, an odd feeling began to grow in him.

This *was* his boat and, because of that, these were his men.

Peter had never felt exactly this way while Jonesy had been alive and *Slewfoot* had been Jonesy's boat. He had felt then—and the men must feel this now—that his life was in Jones's hands. The boat and everything in it were the responsibility of Jones.

Sitting in the dark there this feeling got pretty big. Peter looked around at the men resting in dark heaps on the deck, and thought about the others below—the motormacs in their inferno, the cook who would now be trying to dish up something for the midnight change of the watch. All of their lives depended on the commanding officer now, depended on his making the right decision.

So this, Peter thought, is what it feels like to be captain of a ship. It awed him and made him feel small and ineffective.

The radarman poked his head out of the hatch and said, "Bogeys, three big ones, course two seven zero, range nine thousand, speed fifteen."

Peter jumped out of the chair, almost dropping the big glasses, and dropped down into the radar shack.

As the thin scanning line of the radar swept slowly around to 270° on the scope it was just a thin, greenish line, but as it hit 270, suddenly three large green bulges appeared, glowed strongly for a second, then faded away.

The radarman said, "*Big* mothers."

Peter just nodded, waiting for the blips to show again.

These were not the enemy's *daihatsu* or even *toku daihatsu* barges which he usually used to move troops and supplies at night. Even the big *daihatsu* could only make 9 knots and these things on the radar were making a good 15.

Peter checked the range and watched the blips come up again.

"They're as big as cruisers," the radarman said. "Maybe carriers."

From behind them Murph said, "Or battlewagons. Want me to send a contact report, skipper?"

"No," Peter said, watching the screen. This surprised

Murphy. It was essential that the Base know if any PT made a contact because it might be the last thing the Base ever heard from that boat. It said in big print in the book: RADIO BASE IMMEDIATELY ON MAKING CONTACT WITH THE ENEMY.

Then Murphy had a thought he didn't want to think. It just came into his mind, unbidden and unwelcome. If Peter sent no contact report there would be no record of contact. The three enemy ships could slide on through the night, undetected, unmolested. Peter and all the men in the boat could just pretend they had not seen a thing.

For those ships were big and fast and tough.

"Ask Mitch to come aft," Peter said, and went out to the bridge. As he stepped up beside Murphy and peered into the darkness, he suddenly felt more alone than he had ever felt in his life. "I'll take it," he told Murph, wanting badly to have something to do.

The enemy ships were on a course due west, heading straight toward New Guinea as they sailed along the curving coast of New Britain. *Slewfoot* was between them and New Britain so that the landmass of the island made it impossible for the enemy radar to detect the boat. Peter was sure that, now, the enemy had no idea that he was so close. But Peter knew he could not make an attack on them without sailing clear of the land on his beam. At the speed they were making he would have to take *Slewfoot* out across the Dampier Strait and the instant he did, the enemy radars would light up like Christmas.

Mitchell, the big bosun, appeared out of the darkness. "You want me, skipper?"

"We've got three bogeys, big as cruisers," Peter said, pointing in the direction of the invisible enemy. "See if you can make 'em out." He handed Mitch the big glasses.

Mitch went aft and climbed up on top of the tank compartments. Murph, with a pair of 7 by 30 glasses, was already up there.

"See anything?" Mitch asked.

"Black as your heart," Murph said.

"Well, why doesn't he close in on 'em?" Mitch asked.

Murph looked at the big bosun in the darkness. Murph was thinking the same thing but he wasn't going to give the big ape the satisfaction of running down the skipper.

"He's biding his time," Murph said.

"He's letting 'em get away," Mitch said.

"So you want to run over there and get blown out of the water before we even see 'em?"

Mitch looked down at him scornfully. "Jonesy would have been on his way by now. *On his way.*"

Then Murph saw them and it chilled him. The black silhouettes moving across the sea were *enormous*. Long, and black, and high hulled. Enormous.

Murph climbed down and ran to the bridge, handing Peter the glasses. "They're battleships. Anyway, cruisers."

Peter scanned the sea, stopped, looked. The sight chilled him, too. The huge ships seemed to fill the whole horizon. He handed the glasses back to Murphy. "Transports," he said. "Attack transports."

"Want me to pass the word for battle stations?" Murph asked.

"No," Peter said.

Murph stood in the dark, staring at him. If this man had been Jonesy things would have been different now. *Slewfoot* would have been on her way toward those enemy ships, her engines wide open. Every man would have been at his battle station; the torpedomen would have been setting the fish to go.

Instead, Peter held *Slewfoot* on a course away from the enemy and half the crew lay asleep on the deck.

"Take it," Peter said, stepping aside for Murphy to take the wheel.

Through the black night Peter stood and looked at the huge ships through the binoculars. Big and black and ominous, not a light showing, not a sound coming from them.

Estimate of the Situation. That's what they called it in the Navy school. Estimate of the Situation. Where was the enemy? How strong was he? What would he probably do? What could he do that you could not expect? What will you do if he does so-and-so? Finally, what can you *make* him do?

There was no doubt about where the enemy was, and where he was going and what he would probably do if attacked. And it looked as though his strength was three big, armed, fast transports.

This, Peter decided, was the first problem. The enemy sometimes sent their *daihatsu* barges out on the sea with no other protection than the guns they carried, the darkness and, usually, rain. But would the enemy be so foolish as to send three of his biggest and best and scarcest attack transports with only deck guns and darkness for protection? The enemy knew, by bitter losses, that U. S. PT boats nightly prowled the waters he was now sailing in. Would he send three immensely valuable ships out here with nothing to fight off the PTs?

Peter didn't think so. There must be destroyers convoying these transports. There *had* to be, but where *were* they?

Without knowing the answer to that he could not go on with his estimate of the situation. He leaned down into the radar shack and said, "Take a good look all around, Willie."

In a moment Willie reported, "Three bogeys is all I see."

Where *were* they? "Hold course," he told Murph and then swung down into the radar shack, motioning Willie off the high stool. As he reached for the controls he noticed that his hands were shaking and wondered why. He didn't feel any more afraid than usual. Frustration at not knowing what he wanted to know, he thought, or just plain excitement.

Mitch, the bosun, went by the shack and looked down and saw Peter's hands shaking.

Jonesy's hands had never shaken like that in a fight, Mitch thought. *Never.* He stepped up beside Murph and whispered, "The Exec's hands are shaking like a leaf."

"You'd be shaking, too," Murph said. But it bothered him, hurt him. He had thought a lot of Peter. Next to Jones, Peter Brent had been top man. And when Jonesy was alive he had never seen Peter act the way he was acting now—undecided, confused and shaking. Peter had always seemed just as brave —well, almost as brave—as Jones. Now he was down in the radar shack shaking and letting the enemy get away.

Peter studied the blips the enemy ships made on the screen. He couldn't be sure, but occasionally they seemed to change in size, just a little, getting a little bigger now, and then a little smaller. He couldn't be sure, but it was the only way he could explain it.

The Estimate of the Situation, the professor had said, was simply an educated guess. Now, Peter thought, I've got to go on with the rest of the problem using a pretty wild guess.

He climbed out of the shack to the bridge where Mitch slowly moved aside for him. "Mitch," Peter said, "stand by to make smoke."

In the darkness the big bosun stared at Peter with surprise and then disgust. Up to now, Mitch thought, it had been bad, but this was downright sickening. Mumbling under his breath, he went aft. Stucky, the 40-millimeter Bofors gunner, was lying asleep on the deck and the sight of him gave Mitch something to pour his anger out on. He kicked Stucky in the stern and as Stucky came up fighting Mitch shoved him down with one big paw.

"What's up?" Stucky asked.

"We've got three big ships out there we could run in on and sink—wham wham wham. So what are we doing? We're running away. I'm going to make some smoke now before we even get shot at."

Stucky couldn't believe it. "What's the skipper doing?"

"The *Exec*," Mitch said scornfully, "is so scared he's hanging onto the wheel so he won't fall down."

"Mr. Brent? Mr. Brent's scared?"

"And I thought he'd make a good skipper," Mitch said, as he moved on to the smoke generator.

This was a large steel drum on the after end of the boat. The smoke was not true smoke, but a chemical mixture under pressure in the drum, which, when released, poured out over the water and hung thick and heavy and evil smelling—a wall of smoke. Mitch set the valves and made sure the release lanyards were clear and then sat down beside Stucky.

"As soon as we hit the beach I'm putting in for a transfer off this boat," Mitch told him. "It's bad enough in the boats with a guy like Jones. But I'm not riding with a kid so scared he can't stand up."

"Well, this is his first time as skipper," Stucky argued.

"It doesn't take but one time for a man to show what's up his back," Mitch said.

As he did, the engines in the compartment directly below him increased their muffled roar until the whine of the superchargers could no longer be subdued.

"Maybe you're wrong," Stucky said. "Looks like we're going in."

For a moment it did look that way, but *Slewfoot* kept turning, turning past a course that would have sent her to the enemy, turning almost 180° before she settled back on course.

"That does it," Mitch said. "Now he's not only running away, he's running for home."

On the bridge Murph, standing beside Peter, asked, "Are we going home?"

"I hope so," Peter said. "Get all the deckhands up here, Murph."

Murph went forward and woke up the sleeping gunners and torpedomen. "The skip . . . Mr. Brent wants to talk to you," he told them. Then he went aft and gathered up Mitch and the gunners back there.

"What do we get now—alibis?" Mitch asked.

Murph was too sick at heart to answer.

The men gathered at the bridge and stood in silence, looking up at Peter on the steering platform.

Peter turned the wheel over to Murph and turned to face the men.

"There's more out there than we can handle," he told them in a low voice. "Three big transports with five-inch guns and all the troop machine guns and small arms . . ."

Mitch interrupted him: "We've got four torpedoes. That's one more than we need for a little job like this."

"Theoretically," Peter agreed. "But I think there's more to it than that, so I'm going to leave the transports for the other boats."

Murphy couldn't believe it. He looked at Peter in the dark and now Peter seemed to be someone he had never seen before. "You're going to let 'em get away?" Murph asked.

"We're going to have to. Send a contact report to all boats on patrol that three big transports are coming their way."

It made the bosun sick. "If the other boats can take 'em on, why can't we?"

"Because I don't know what's out there," Peter said. "So go aft and get that generator ready to jettison."

"Jettison?" Mitch almost yelled. "What do you mean, *jettison?*"

"Just that," Peter told him. "If I pass the word, start making smoke and then be ready to jettison."

Mitch was so close to mutiny that he was afraid to stand there in front of Peter any longer. "Okay," he said. "You're the boss . . . the book says."

Mitch moved aft and said to Stucky on the Bofors, "Chicken. Pure chicken. And not only that, he lets 'em ride right down on the other boats."

"I don't understand it," Stucky agreed. "The least we could do is make a run on 'em. Shake 'em up a little."

As Mitch moved on to the smoke generator and started unbolting it he said, "I'm never going to ride in a boat with that guy again. Even if I have to gundeck something I'm never going to ride a boat with Ensign Peter Brent, USN—R."

4

Estimate of the Situation: The enemy was *there*, a few thousand yards to the starboard of *Slewfoot*; the enemy's mission was crystal clear: carry troops and supplies to New Guinea; the enemy's strength?

Peter looked over at the dark ships moving on the dark sea with the dark sky behind them.

The enemy's strength?

There was nothing Peter could do until he found the answer to that. And there was only one way to do it.

The risk and the danger of what he now had to do appalled him. Once embarked on the maneuver the end result would be simply life or death for *Slewfoot* and the men in her.

There was one small consolation for Peter. It was in the hands of the enemy whether *Slewfoot* lived or died, but the enemy's decision would have to be made in a matter of *seconds*. The enemy would have to think fast and shoot fast in those seconds because *Slewfoot* was going to be *moving* when the time came.

Peter put on a pair of goggles with deep-red lenses so the lights below decks would not ruin his night vision when he came back to the bridge. "I'm going below," he told Murph. "Hold her steady."

"Steady as she goes," Murph said.

Peter dropped down the hatch and went through the crew's space to the engine room. On deck you could barely hear the engines—it was really more of a feeling than a sound

—but when Peter opened the little door through the fire wall and crawled into Sko's inferno the sound was monstrous.

Sko was sitting in his tractor seat above the center engine with one foot on each of the outboard engines. He was naked to the waist and sweat was pouring from him and dripping in a steady little stream from the end of a big, unlighted cigar he had clamped in his teeth. That was a bad sign, Peter knew, because Sko never chomped on that cigar unless he was worried.

Peter explained what was going on and then asked, "How they running, Sko?"

"Pretty good, skipper. But they sure need an overhaul."

"Pretty soon they've got to go from a dead stop to full out," Peter told him. "Will they do it?"

Sko shrugged and scraped the sweat off his elbows. "We can try," he said, "but if they gulp one time we're dead." He patted one of the engines with his foot. "Particularly Betsy, here. She's been cantankerous for a week."

"Talk nice to her," Peter said and went out.

Sko turned to the two motormacs down on the hot steel decking. "Listen, you swab handles!" he yelled at them. "When you see those accelerator rods begin to move, give these girls just a little tickle—just a *little*. And if I hear a single cylinder gulp so help me I'll shove you out the exhaust pipe."

"All you will hear will be a faint scream of indignation," the Professor said.

The Professor, whose real name was John B. White, was nineteen, but he had had a year of college and was *very smart*. He stood now smiling sweetly at Sko until Sko turned back to the control panel and clutches. Then the Professor turned on Skeeter, the other motormac, and said, "You heard His Majesty?"

"I heard," Skeeter said, "and tomorrow I put in for a transfer off this rusty bucket of bolts. *Nobody* can call me swab handle. I'm *Mr.* Swab Handle."

When Peter got back to the bridge and took off the goggles he found that Murph, intentionally or not, had closed the course so that *Slewfoot* was now less than six thousand yards from the dark, speeding transports. For a moment Peter felt a hot flash of anger—if they spotted *Slewfoot* now . . . blooey—but he controlled it and said, "Nothing to the right, Murph. From *now on*."

"Nothing to the right," Murph said, and then added, "Why don't we let 'em have just one fish? Just for the fun of it."

"We're leaving them alone," Peter told him firmly. Then he went over to the gunners. "You guys on the guns, listen. When I say 'Fire' I want ten rounds from the machine guns and two rounds apiece from the twenties and the forty. Then *stop*. Not another shot—no matter what happens."

"Even searchlights?" Jason asked.

"Not another shot—lights or no lights."

Stucky, on the 40, asked, "What are we going to shoot *at*?"

"Nothing," Peter said.

Shaking his head, Stucky went aft to where Mitch was sitting gloomily on the smoke generator. "I think he's lost his mind," Stucky said.

"If he ever had one. Oh, what Jonesy would have done with a setup like this! If Jonesy was here we'd've sunk 'em all by now."

"Shooting at nothing," Stucky said vaguely. "Wait till the taxpayers hear about this."

On the bridge Peter turned and looked over at the dark mass of New Britain. The island was running out fast, sloping from the mountains down to the point at the entrance of Dampier Strait. A tiny flicker of light over there marked the little town with the cute name, Sag-Sag. Peter had always thought that was a fine name for a town.

In a moment now there would be no more island to absorb *Slewfoot's* image on the enemy's radar. In a moment he was going to get the answer.

To keep the engines from choking up on an abrupt change of speed, Peter throttled back slowly to idle and, at the same time, called aft to Mitch, "Make smoke."

As Mitch turned the generator on he laughed a little sourly. "We're going to fight dem skeeters all de way home. Ain't we *brave?*" he said to Stucky.

The thick, acrid smoke gushed out of the tubes, flowed down heavily over the stern, and then striking the water, flowed out over it, slowly rising. To Peter, watching it, it looked as though *Slewfoot* were leaving behind a solid gray wall, thick and high.

Peter let it flow out for a hundred yards and then buzzed Sko to reverse all engines. When he felt the props bite he told Murphy to back her straight into the smoke.

The stuff was thick and crummy, burning their skins a little and making them cough as Murph backed the boat slowly into it. Peter watched until the smoke curved around the bow and *Slewfoot* was entirely in it. Then he said, quietly, "Commence firing."

It was weird. At one moment *Slewfoot* was an invisible thing inside the pall of thick smoke. In the next she was a fiercely glowing, flickering, flaming mass of brilliance as all her guns began to fire, the tracers going out through the smoke like thin chains of light. The thick smoke around her glowed with a wavering, eerie light as though the light itself were holding her.

And from a silent boat she was now a roaring, chattering, hammering, thudding explosion of sound.

In the engine room Sko waited, listening to the uproar above him. To him the oddest sound in all the noise of a fight was the sharp clatter of the brass empties falling on the deck. It sounded to him like some sort of hellish rain.

Sko looked back at the Professor and Skeeter but didn't have to say anything. Somehow, down here in the engine room where you couldn't see and nobody ever told you, you knew, somehow, when the moment of danger was at hand.

Sko and Skeeter and the Professor knew it now—and waited.

It only took a few seconds to get off the ten rounds from the machine guns and those were the only seconds Peter was going to give his enemy to make his decision. That he would shoot, you could count on. Shells from the big guns were on the way now, Peter knew, streaking toward him through the dark sky, whirling as they came.

"Jettison smoke generator!" he yelled aft to Mitch.

Mitch was really scared now. Not of the enemy—he'd seen him before—but of Peter and what Peter was doing. To stop a PT boat dead in the water so that she was a perfect target and *then* open fire was insane.

The uproar of the guns stopped as suddenly as it had begun, the ten rounds spent. Mitch rolled the smoke drum over the stern, and in the sudden silence the splash sounded as though it could be heard all the way to New Guinea.

Jason, the gunner, lifted his head from the warm sighting rest and turned to look anxiously at Peter. Welborn, the Preacher, turned from his torpedo racks to look at Peter.

Sko sat silent above his engines, the cigar finally motionless; the Professor and Skeeter stood on the hot plates and watched the accelerator rods as the big engines ticked over slowly.

Peter saw the smoke generator roll upright in the water and saw the smoke rolling out of it.

And then he heard them coming. In the silent night, with only the purr of the idling engines he could actually hear the high, approaching scream of the enemy's shells.

In almost a single smooth movement Peter rang for ahead, emergency, and began to move the three throttles forward. At the same time, instinctively, for he had always handled the wheel in a fight when Jones was skipper, he stepped to the wheel.

And then he stood there with nothing to do but wait.

The engines would either take it or they would not. They would roll or falter.

Sko listened to those three engines as though he were a part of them. In his body he could feel the crankshafts beginning to *move* as the pistons began the furious sliding in the oiled cylinders. He turned his head aft and looked for a second at the series of belts on the V-drives of the outboard engines, and then he looked down at Skeeter and the Professor and they too were now a part of the engines.

Peter waited, the screaming on top of him now, waited for the power to pour through the reduction gears and on into the bronze shafts and out through the shaft logs to the bronze propellers and, finally, to strike the water.

The whole boat was rammed sideways through the water as the enemy salvo struck close abeam and exploded. Men who were not holding on were thrown down; those who were, almost had their grips broken by the force of it.

And then, almost invisible in the smoke, the mountain of water fell out of nowhere on *Slewfoot*. It washed the fallen men helplessly across the deck, drenched all hands, and struck Peter full in the face, nearly knocking him away from the wheel.

Sko looked at the bulkheads and the ceiling close above him. He was looking for the black sea to come in there with him.

Sam, the cook, got up off the deck of the dayroom and ran forward to see if the boat had been holed around the bow.

The men got up, one by one, and went back to the guns and racks.

But, now, *Slewfoot* was under way. As Peter wiped the salt water out of his eyes, he looked ahead through the smoke and saw the long, slim bow coming up. And he felt the stern squatting, felt the shove of the engines rocking him back.

Sko watched his tachometers, the thin needles moving steadily across the faces of the dials, 1900, 2000, 2500. For this one time, Sko decided, let 'em go to the pegs.

"I'm sorry, little girls," he said to the engines, "but we need it *all*."

On the bridge Peter said to Murph, "When we break out of this smoke we're going to be headed straight for New Britain. Let's don't go aground."

A salvo of shells came whining down through the smoke and struck somewhere behind *Slewfoot*, throwing up another geyser of water.

And then the smoke thinned and *Slewfoot* came tearing out of it, trailing little tendrils of the thick stuff for a moment until the wind of her movement blew it clear.

In the abrupt change from the dense smoke to the clear air it seemed for a few seconds as though the dark island was on top of them. Peter threw the wheel hard over, *Slewfoot* spinning hard in the turn and throwing up a long, curling slice of white water.

He straightened her out, moving close beside the island, and now she ran, the mufflers off the big Packards, the tach needles up against the pegs, the superchargers screaming.

He was on a parallel course with the enemy again and had no trouble making him out. Every searchlight on each of the transports was blazing, the deck cannon were shooting with frightening speed, the muzzle blasts like blinking lights in a sign. And all along the decks of the ships the troop machine guns and rifles were blazing away, tiny winking lights.

They were giving that smoke a beating. The searchlights were playing back and forth along the length of it. The tracers were pouring into it like streams of light.

Peter turned then and looked at the island on his left. Now he could see the tiny, dim spots of light in the town of Sag-Sag—firefly glows made by the oil lamps of the natives.

Speed was all he had now as the land ran out and *Slewfoot* tore across the wide entrance of Dampier Strait—speed and the smoke that was still being made by the floating generator. Let them probe that with their radars, he thought.

The situation was now this: the three transports had not changed course or speed as they searched the smoke cloud with their lights and shells. *Slewfoot*, with the Packards all out, was ahead of the transports now, six thousand yards to the left of them and on the same course.

Peter kept waiting for the radarman to say something, and as time passed and no word came, he began to wonder if he had made a mistake. Had his estimate of the situation been completely wrong?

If it was wrong then what he had done was about as wrong as you could make it. He had given away to the enemy the priceless thing a PT boat had—surprise. They knew now that they were under attack, and now, because of what he had done, they were ready for him.

"Take it," he said to Murph. "Nothing to the right."

Peter dropped down into the radar shack and looked over Willie's shoulder.

"I was just going to call you," Willie said. "There's something fishy. See how those blips are changing? They look like they're getting bigger."

Peter looked at them and the relief he felt was almost solid.

In a moment there were not three blips, there were four . . . five . . . six.

He had to give the enemy credit for a smart maneuver. The destroyers must have been sailing almost within shouting distance of the transports and right alongside and to seaward so that a PT boat, hugging the land, could not see them either by radar or binoculars.

A beautiful trap, Peter decided.

Murph's head appeared in the hatch and his voice was up three notches. "Cans, skipper! Three destroyers!"

"I know," Peter said, coming out of the shack.

Jason saw them then and said, "Holy mack-e-rel, Amos!"

Mitch, the big bosun, coming forward saw them and stopped in his tracks. "My God! Look at that!"

The Preacher saw them and backed away a few steps as though the three destroyers were menacing him with a fist.

Peter said to Murph, "Send a contact report—all boats. Three cans, three transports. Base course two seven zero, speed fifteen, now abeam Umboi Island at fifteen thousand yards." Then he spun *Slewfoot* around in a wide flat disk of spray until she was heading straight back toward the destroyers.

The destroyers were moving too. Peter could see the white wakes streaming as, in a column, they drove toward the low cloud of smoke still lit by the searchlights. Then either a destroyer or a transport started firing flares that burst high above the smoke and hung up there, brilliant swaying lights that seemed to light the sea and the smoke and the destroyers as though on a stage. Against these lights the details of *Slewfoot* seemed cut out of pure blackness—every man and object silhouetted and without dimension.

Down in the engine room Sko and Skeeter and the Professor waited in the solid sound and heat and terrible vibration of the big engines.

Sam, the cook, with nothing to do for the moment, ducked below and ran aft to the engine room. "Three destroyers," he yelled at Sko.

"Shooting at us?" Sko yelled back.

"Not yet, but soon, man, soon."

On the bridge Murph was trying to read the bearing, hanging on with all his might against the hard, slamming, pitching, bucking, slithering of *Slewfoot* as she gathered speed after the turn and worked up past 45 knots. She was throwing white spray all over the ocean, and a huge, rolling foothill of churned water rose as though carved solid just abaft the stern.

"What's the range?" Peter yelled down to the radarman.

"Six thousand."

Peter looked at the scene ahead of him—the three enormous transports, the superstructure and decks sharply lit by the muzzle flashes and searchlights. And at the three destroyers, all lights blazing, guns now firing into the cloud of smoke. Above and ahead of the destroyers the flares hung like hard white suns in the black sky.

Slewfoot could turn now, turn away in her dark world and, engines muffled again, sneak away through the Strait and those six ships of the enemy would never find her.

Or she could go on as she was going—the exhaust a solid thunder, the crack of water against the sharp bow like stones striking together—go on to the enemy.

5

The young- est man aboard *Slewfoot* was a seventeen-year-old who had lied about his age to get in the Navy. That morning he had sneaked into the jungle with a helmet full of water and the razor. He had had to pay five dollars for a 69¢ secondhand razor and to put up with a lot of noise about wiping his face with a wet towel but, in the jungle where no one could see him, he had decided he needed a razor. Putting the metal signaling mirror he had liberated from a life raft up in the fork of a bush, he had studied himself carefully and decided that what looked like fuzz to the other men was, actually, a beard. He had shaved it slowly and carefully, washed the razor and hidden it.

His name was Bridgers, but the crew of *Slewfoot* called him Britches—or Kid, or Baby, or Mother's Boy, or worse—and now he was so scared his eyes were swimming as he stood beside his torpedo rack and looked ahead at the speeding destroyers. What he wanted now—more than anything he had ever wanted in his life—was just to talk to somebody, just to feel that he wasn't all alone out here. But Goldberg, the torpedoman, was standing beside him staring at the enemy and didn't look as though he wanted to talk.

Goldberg was a big, hulking, forbidding man whose voice sounded as though it were coming through a bucket of gravel. There were times when you could talk to Goldberg and times when you'd better not. But Britches was lonely and he decided to risk it. "Big, aren't they?" he asked, trying not to let his voice squeak, but it did anyway.

"Medium size," Goldberg graveled at him.

Talking didn't seem to help Britches' fear much—it had grown absolutely solid and alive and a lot bigger than he was. "Do you think Mr. Brent's going to attack 'em?" he asked.

"If he isn't we'd sure better get off this course."

"Do you think he should?" Britches asked. "Aren't they . . . I mean . . . well, look at 'em."

"I'm looking at 'em."

Britches asked, "Are you scared, Goldberg?"

"Scared? Who, me?" Goldberg growled, and then he looked down at Britches. "I'm too scared to be scared. You never fought a destroyer, did you? You never had one shooting right down your throat, did you? You've just been fooling around knocking off those helpless barges. Well, if he keeps on going in this way you just wait, sonny boy, just wait. It's going to be the biggest Fourth of July you ever saw. Man, I remember one time in The Slot . . ."

Britches had just wanted to talk to somebody, but as Goldberg went on and on he decided that this was the next best thing—to have somebody talk to him.

On the other torpedo rack the Preacher stood and looked ahead and wondered how men did it. How had Jonesy had the courage to do the things he had done? And now, how did Mr. Brent have the courage? Was there something in being an officer that gave you courage? The Preacher didn't think so. It was just something some men had. Some didn't. The Preacher knew that if he were skipper now he would turn

Slewfoot on her screws and run. There were too many destroyers, too many guns, too many *everything* for one PT boat to take on alone.

Jason, the gunner, looked at the ships ahead of him all bathed in the brilliant light, and it seemed to him that he was alone in a dark world and those ships were sliding sideways toward him.

Jason could feel his mouth beginning to get dry, felt the shakes crawling toward him across the deck. But he knew what to do about that. He leaned in against his guns, jamming his shoulders into the curved braces and then he swung them toward the destroyers and looked at the ships now through the ring sight of his guns. This way the ships were no longer the enemy, no longer a threat to him. They were just a target.

Stucky on the big Bofors cannon looked at the destroyers. They were shooting now with everything that would bear —sheets of tracers pouring into the rolling cloud of smoke the floating generator was still sending up. The AA guns were banging away, the long barrels pumping back and forth like pistons. The muzzles of the machine guns seemed to be on fire. The turret guns were shooting more slowly and it interested Stucky to watch how the gout of flame would suddenly appear—flame and smoke—but the destroyers were going so fast, the wind was whipping the smoke straight back down the outside of the barrels. Stucky decided he wouldn't like to work in a turret gun, wouldn't like being cooped up inside that steel room with nothing to see except the big breech of the gun lunging back at you.

Mitch watched the destroyers and decided that there were good gunners behind all those guns. Gunners who could get on target fast and clamp you in a straddle of shells you couldn't get through alive.

The radarman stuck his head out of the hatch and looked at the enemy. They were so different from the little green blips on the scope. On his radar they seemed real, now they didn't.

There wasn't a man on *Slewfoot* who wanted to press an attack on those ships, nor a man who would admit it.

The radarman called up to Peter, "Range five thousand," and went back to the scope to look at the blips again.

Murph, who was trying to take bearings, looked over at Peter. Nobody would blame the skipper, Murph decided, if he turned away now and got out of here. After all . . . three big destroyers . . .

Mitch said to Stucky on the 40-millimeter, "What's he doing? I tell you, he's out of his mind. We're going to get our heads blown off."

"What's the matter, Mitch, you want to live forever?"

"I sure do."

The radarman said, "Range four thousand."

Murphy watched Peter as he wiped the spray out of his eyes. It was now or never, Murph decided.

Peter leaned over to Goldberg on the starboard torpedo racks and said, "Give the lead destroyer both fish, Gerry. Set depth five feet, speed high."

Goldberg looked up at him. "You going to shoot from here, skipper?"

Peter hesitated for a moment. Murph couldn't decide whether it was to think, or just spit some spray out of his mouth. Then Peter said, "No. We're going all the way, Gerry." Then he leaned over to port and said to the Preacher, "Give the next two, one apiece, Preacher."

Beside the engine controls was a target data computer—elemental compared to those on submarines, but good enough to give you a collision course between the target and the torpedo. Peter studied it now as he said, "Keep the bearings coming, Murph."

The radarman called up, "Range three thousand, skipper."

Peter looked ahead at the target, now only a mile away. Apparently the transports had stopped firing flares, for no more of them were blossoming in the sky and the last of them were falling through the smoke into the sea.

Suddenly, as though done with a master switch, all the searchlights on both the destroyers and the transports went out and, at the same time, all the guns stopped firing.

It was done so suddenly and completely that the ships ahead of him seemed to Peter to have vanished, leaving nothing behind but a solid black wave of darkness which was rolling across the sea toward him.

Peter leaned over to Goldberg. "Set both fish right five degrees, Gerry."

"Five right," Goldberg said and Britches jumped to the manual controls.

Peter leaned to the left. "Preacher, set number one left three, number two left six."

"One left three, two left six," the Preacher said.

"Stand by on the guns," Peter called out.

Peter could still see nothing ahead of him, his eyes still unadjusted to the sudden total darkness. "Murph," he said to the shadowy little man beside him, "if anything happens, take over and try to get the fish off as close to a thousand yards as you can. Then get the boat back into the smoke and get her into the Siassi Strait. They can't follow you through there."

"Range two thousand," the radarman called up.

Murph said, "If they spot us and start shooting, are we going to go on in to a thousand?"

"I think we should," Peter said. "I guess that's what we're here for."

"I guess so," Murph said.

And then the lights came on. They were like long thin knives stabbing you through the eyes, stabbing right on through your brain. There was nothing you could do—the knives sliced through your lids if you tried to shut them out by closing your eyes.

And this time the lights were on *Slewfoot* and she, instead of the destroyers, was in the center of the brilliant stage, the searchlights seeming to hold her as though the beams were solid and unbreakable.

Every detail on *Slewfoot* was suddenly sharp and clear and bright, every drop of water she threw, shining like a jewel.

Peter's first instinct was to put the wheel hard over and break *Slewfoot* out of the grip of those lights, or at least zigzag her, but he held her steady as she went—waiting.

The terrible game was starting now, the guessing game. Guess wrong and you died.

Behind the brilliance of the searchlights he could not see the muzzle flash as the ships began firing at *Slewfoot*, so that when the first salvo hit, it startled him, the tower of bright white water rising to the left.

The guessing game. They had missed you and were correcting their aim now to hit you. If you held course, the next salvo would blow you out of the water.

Peter swung *Slewfoot* toward the falling column of water, and as her wake curved, a salvo fell squarely into it.

Guess again. He swung her back, hard.

Now the sea all around the boat was like a forest of weird white growing and dying trees as the shells struck and exploded, the gouts of water plunging upward, then falling.

"Fifteen hundred," the radarman yelled.

"Get those lights!" Peter yelled at the gunners. They were trying. Every gun on *Slewfoot* that would bear was pounding, the tracers streaking away, but fifteen hundred yards is a long way to hit a three-foot target from a boat moving at 50 miles an hour through a rain of gunfire. The six searchlights continued to blaze.

On the destroyers, the smaller caliber guns opened up so that in the air between *Slewfoot* and the target the streams of tracers coming and going looked like a cat's cradle made of blazing dotted strings.

Peter hurled the boat from side to side, twisting and turning through the forest of waterspouts. In his mind he tried to remember the turns and the duration of them and the courses so that when the fatal time came he could drop her fast and surely on the base course.

That was the terrible time, and all hands were waiting for it—the time when you had to hold her on course and let her settle down to the rhythm of the sea and go straight in on the enemy until you reached the firing point and the torpedoes left the racks. And even then there would be a few more seconds of that time, while the torpedoes splashed into the sea and began to run. You had to wait until they were clear before you could turn and leave that place.

Jason was shoving against the shoulder pads trying to add his own strength to the bullets streaming from the twin barrels, trying to give them that extra inch they needed to reach the lights.

And he began to reach them. One of them stopped blazing and burned for a few seconds with a sick weak yellowness before going out, but Jason had already swung his guns to the next one.

Peter looked down at the flux gate and swung *Slewfoot* over onto the base course. "Base course!" he yelled at the torpedomen. "Stand by to fire torpedoes."

Gerry Goldberg looked down at Britches. The kid was just standing there, looking ahead, both hands on the rack. A searchlight beam was directly on him and he was squinting against it. Suddenly Goldberg leaned down closer, inspecting the boy. "Hey," he said, "you been shaving?"

"Doesn't everybody?" Britches asked.

It broke up Goldberg.

Peter, listening to Goldberg's laughing, wondered what was so funny and made a note to ask Goldberg, when this was over. He leaned down into the radar shack and said, "Keep 'em coming in hundreds now, Willie."

"Twelve hundred," Willie said.

The salvos were closing in on *Slewfoot* now as she settled on the base course and no longer weaved and dodged.

Like two closing walls of almost solid water they were walking in toward her.

Mitch, feeding shells to the Bofors, said, "This is the longest ride I ever took."

In the engine room Sko felt the boat steady down. "Here we go," he said.

Skeeter, the motormac third, said, "Why doesn't something happen?"

The Professor reminded him, "They also serve who only stand and wait, Skeeter."

"Eleven hundred," the radarman yelled just before a tower of water fell squarely on top of the boat, drowning everything for a moment, and then flowed away, leaving the gun barrels hissing steam.

"One thousand!" Willie yelled.

"Fire! Let 'em go!"

Goldberg and Britches on the starboard side flipped the racks outboard and saw the long oily fish shoot out and forward and splash into the sea. "Run, you little babies. Run!" Goldberg yelled at them. "Run!" Britches yelled, his voice a weak little squeak.

The Preacher called up to the bridge, "Port-side fish gone away."

Peter spun the wheel hard to starboard and as *Slewfoot* leaned and turned, a savage salvo landed exactly where she would have been if she had stayed on course another second.

Now with all her torpedoes in the water *Slewfoot* had nothing left with which she could hurt the destroyers. All she could do now was to try to save her own life.

As she fled for the smoke she was broadside to the destroyers, totally exposed to their guns and still held in the grip of their lights.

Jason looked ahead for a second at the wall of smoke so vague, so far away. Then he looked through his sights again at the three destroyers and they seemed to him to be only a few yards away.

Somehow the shells that were being fired at him did not bother Jason. To him they were just something that caused towers of water to rise from the flat sea all around him. To Jason the lights were the enemy, the hard, blazing, unwinking eyes of the searchlights.

One by one the searchlights went out, the dark, invisible bullets following in the path of the tracers, until Jason could find no more to aim his guns at.

Now only the sides of the destroyers showed light of any sort and that was a mean flickering, dotted with larger gouts from the turrets.

"Good shooting," Peter yelled down to him.

With the lights gone, Peter began to think that they were going to reach the smoke alive. Salvos were still landing all around the boat and the tracers were either floating close over his head or falling short, striking the water and sizzling out.

He was counting off the seconds of the torpedo run, ". . . eight . . . Missouri . . . nine . . ." when it happened.

He was looking ahead across the dark sea at the faraway cloud of smoke when the gray-white wall rose directly in front of him, and kept on rising, higher and higher.

He tried to wheel her, but it was too close. "Hang on!" he yelled, and then she hit it.

Slewfoot was going very fast, half her forward hull out of the water, bow high, the three Packards ramming every ounce of their power into the propellers. As Peter yanked the wheel over with one hand, he yanked all three throttles back.

It was too late. The boat hit the column of water almost bows on still traveling at high speed. It was like striking a stone wall. The shock of it tore men loose from their grips and slung them back along the deck. The force of the impact ripped the port torpedo racks, still flipped over, clean off the boat. Water bent the steel struts of the gun mounts and then struck the bridge structure, cracking it open, tearing off the windshield as it poured over the top.

Solid, racing water slammed against the tank compartments poured down into the radar shack, rushed on aft to crash against the Bofors and the depth charges, almost drowning Stucky and Mitch who were hiding behind them.

Then it poured off the stern and *Slewfoot* was left motionless in the water, stopped in her tracks.

As Peter rammed the throttles forward again, he yelled, "Anybody hurt?" as he watched the dark forms of men getting slowly to their feet.

"I guess not," Goldberg said, untangling Britches from the starboard racks. "But let's don't do that again."

As *Slewfoot* began to gather speed, Peter yelled to Britches to go below and see if she was taking water.

In the engine compartment Skeeter and the Professor were getting up off the hot deck, Sko was climbing back into his tractor seat. "Guess we caught one," Skeeter said, reaching up for a life jacket as he headed for the door.

"Get back to your engine!" Sko yelled at him. "Nobody leaves here as long as they're running."

Peter counted out loud as he wove her through the forest: ". . . fourteen . . . Missouri . . . fifteen . . ."

Britches stuck his head out of the hatch and called, "Don't see any water coming in, Captain."

Peter waved acknowledgment and went on counting, and began to wonder if he had made a mistake. The torpedoes were moving at 33 knots on a range a little over a thousand yards. They should be getting there, or they had missed.

In the darkness he could just make out the outline of the destroyers and saw them turning toward him. Not directly, but on a course that would block him from reaching the smoke.

" . . . Missouri . . ." Peter counted, "eighteen . . ."

The lead destroyer, turning hard to starboard, was throwing a huge white wave when Peter saw the weird glow beginning in her hull—low and dim and far down. It was, at first, just a dull, spreading patch of orange light which looked to him the way it did when he was a kid and held a flashlight against the palm of his hand.

He watched it, fascinated, as it glowed more brightly and began to spread like a disease in the hull of the ship.

And then the destroyer blew up.

Peter couldn't believe it. Couldn't believe that a living, moving, fighting ship could so suddenly come apart like that.

Great pieces and sections and parts of it hurtled up into the sky and were followed by the yellow-white flame of the explosion. Then everything was smothered in the bloom of smoke, lit from the inside by the flame.

Peter had to give credit to his enemy. The other two destroyers reacted almost instantly, throwing themselves hard around in the water to put their bows toward the oncoming torpedoes. For a moment the two ships concentrated on their own lives.

It was the moment *Slewfoot* needed. She disappeared into the smoke of her own making, raced through it and, in the clear again, was into the Siassi Strait, threading her way through the rocks and shoals where nothing bigger than she could go.

6

Slewfoot

reached the mouth of the Morobe just at dawn. As the sun came up the men looked around at their boat and were sad.

Slewfoot was a mess. The destruction of the port rack had torn away part of the deck and freeboard, leaving long ragged splinters of plywood. Her topside was swept clean—the running lights, signal light, searchlight all gone. The hold-down bolts of the gun turrets had been torn almost free, and the heavy steel struts were bent like wires. The depth charges had been ripped out of the racks and even the Bofors mount was bent.

Murph steered her slowly up the river to the rickety dock the crew had made out of empty gas drums and logs and Mitch jumped over with a line.

As the engines sighed to a stop, so did Sko, collapsing forward against the panel. Skeeter and the Professor, staggering a little, got out of the compartment far enough to fall exhausted into the soaking wet bunks. The rest of the men, moving like things in a bad dream, made their way slowly across the dock and slogged through the mud toward Snob Hill.

As Murph and Mitch were starting to leave, Peter called them back. "Mitch, the One Nineteen boat is going down to Milne Bay. If we don't catch it, it'll be a week, maybe two, before we get another chance. You can sleep all the way. And they've got a good cook."

"Who can sleep with that crew of apes?" Mitch grumbled.

"I thought you liked apes. . . . Murph, I'll go along with Mitch, or those Stateside supply officers won't give us the time of day. As soon as the men get moving again see what you can do patching her up."

The 119 boat was nosing down the river and Peter hailed her, asking for a ride. Mitch, still grumbling, jumped with him to the 119, and as Peter went up on the bridge, Mitch turned to the 119's bosun and said, "I just won the war so now I need a little sleep."

"Welcome, friend," the other bosun said. "Take any bunk on the boat—as long as it's right here on deck. We don't want a hero like you to dry out, so we'll keep you sprinkled with nice salty seawater."

And they sprinkled him all the way to Milne Bay.

Milne Bay was by now far behind the fighting and was, to Peter and Mitch, civilization. There were real wooden buildings, a barbershop, ice cream, hot water, Stateside chow.

Best of all, the PTs mother ship was anchored in Milne Bay with spare parts for the boats.

They had very little time to enjoy it. It took most of the night to round up the things they needed to put *Slewfoot* back into fighting trim. Then it took the rest of the night to get them loaded aboard the 119, ready for a dawn departure.

They did manage to sneak in a breakfast of ham and eggs, pancakes with syrup, waffles with butter, toasted bread, some cereal and honest-to-John real cow's milk—not the powdered stuff you mixed with water in a helmet.

Then just before they left they spent all the money they had at the gedunk stand. They got pogey bait—candy, chewing gum, cigarettes (and huge cigars for Sko to chew when he got nervous)—and soap and toothpaste and brushes, paperback books, shoestrings and web belts, pens and ink and paper. Peter remembered Goldberg's laughing in the middle of the fight about Britches shaving, so he bought Britches a razor and shaving soap and foo-foo juice and a styptic pencil to cure the cuts. Then he bought Murph some deodorant because, as Murph freely admitted, when he got scared he smelled like a billy goat.

On the way back to Morobe, Peter and Mitch sat on the foredeck of the 119, enjoying the sunshine and enjoying having somebody else doing all the work.

"Scuttlebutt says we're moving up pretty soon," Mitch said.

"That's what I heard," Peter said.

"You know, I heard about a guy—I think he was a motormac first, or second—who had orders to join a ship and he never could catch up with her. That guy wandered all over the world trying to catch up with the ship he was supposed to report to. Every time he'd get to a place his ship would've just left for some place else. I guess he's still wandering."

"Join the Navy and see the world," Peter said.

"Maybe that's what we can do," Mitch said.

Peter glanced at him. "That's what we *did*."

"No, I mean, maybe we can just keep moving *Slewfoot* around so that new commanding officer— What's his name— the girl's name?"

"Adrian Archer," Peter said.

"Yeah, him. So he can't ever catch up with us. Like he gets to Morobe and we're up at Madang or Wewak or left New Guinea altogether. He could wander around for months."

"Yeah," Peter said, not paying much attention. He was trying to figure out when was the last time he'd had any sleep—thirty hours ago, forty?

"Then we could just go on like we're going. You could be skipper and Murph can act like exec, unless he gets out of line."

"Yeah," Peter said.

"What do we need with a new captain?" Mitch asked.

Peter finally paid attention to him. "The boat doesn't need any captain at all, Mitch."

Mitch said slowly, "It needs a captain. But not a new one."

"Here comes the rain," Peter said and they moved aft to find a little shelter. Later, Peter wondered if the rain hadn't had a lot to do with what happened. The rain and a sort of delayed reaction after the fight with the destroyers and the no sleep.

Anyway, it happened. It was, of course, raining hard when they got back to the river and nosed up the dripping green tunnel. It was about three o'clock in the afternoon, but it seemed almost night with the jungle and the rain cutting off the sunlight.

Mitch saw it first and for a moment he couldn't believe it. He sat there in a puddle of rain and stared at *Slewfoot*. "Look," he said.

Peter raised his head against the rain and looked.

Slewfoot was tied up to her rickety dock and some repairs had been made, but she still looked a little old, a little tired and pretty beat-up as she floated there in the rain.

On her foredeck was the crew. *Lined up.* In *ranks.*

For Peter the anger started right then. It went all over him like a wave and got stronger and stronger until he couldn't handle it.

There they were: Sko, the Preacher, the Professor, Britches, Sam, Goldberg hulking up in the rain, Murphy shrinking against it, Skeeter and Stucky and Jason and Willie. Lined up. In two stiff ranks. Not dressed in the dungarees torn off above the knees, not in the ragged-sleeved and faded blue shirts, not barefoot.

They were—all of them—standing there in dress whites— white jumpers with the black neckerchiefs bedraggled in the rain; white, bell-bottom trousers; black shoes. And every one of them had his white hat on.

Peter could feel all the training and the discipline and the indoctrination that had turned him into a naval officer holding him back, but it wasn't enough. He knew as he got up and ran forward on the 119 boat and jumped over on *Slewfoot* that he was losing his temper like a little boy, but he couldn't help it.

An officer he had never seen before was standing in front of the men—an officer dressed in creased pants (now the crease was soaking out in the rain) and a creased shirt with the sleeves rolled down, and a black necktie knotted and two-blocked at his throat, and a *cap* with rain running off the shiny black visor and the gold braid glowing with newness even in the dim light. Standing there reading something from a piece of paper.

Peter took him by the shoulder and swung him around and said, his voice shaking with anger, "What's going on around here? What are you doing to my men?" Then he turned the officer loose and faced the crew. Through his rage he saw Murph and Sko and Goldberg shaking their heads in a silent warning but he couldn't stop. "You guys . . . get out of the rain and get out of those clothes." But they just stood there, at attention, in ranks.

Peter turned back to the officer, knowing now who he was. Suddenly all the anger went away, just dribbling out of him and leaving him weak. "Those guys are tired," he said.

"Just who are you?" the officer, a lieutenant junior grade, asked.

Peter looked at him now for the first time. He was a tall, thin man with a thin face and a long thin nose. His eyes were bright, hard blue—to Peter they looked about as sympathetic as a bird's eyes—and he had a tightly set, stubborn mouth and a stubborn, lean chin. He was blond with a fresh washed skin and sandy-colored hair.

"I'm the Exec," Peter said wearily. "Peter Brent."

"Well, Mr. Brent, I have just assumed command of this ship. My name is Archer, Lieutenant Junior Grade Adrian Archer."

All Peter could think of was the old Navy rule: any vessel that can be lifted out of the water and put aboard a ship is a *boat*, not a ship.

"I'm sorry," Peter said.

Archer turned to the men and said, "Secure from quarters." And then he started a saluting movement with his right hand, but none of the men remembered to salute and Archer stood there, his hand half raised.

They started leaving the boat in silence, the white uniforms clinging to them, or slapping wetly around as they walked.

"Hey," Peter called after them, "get changed as soon as you can. We've got this One Nineteen to unload."

Archer stepped in front of him. "Go below, please. There are some things I want to discuss with you."

"Okay," Peter said, "but let's get this stuff unloaded first. We're holding up the One Nineteen boat."

"One of the crew is absent without leave," Archer told him. "Did you know that, Mr. Brent?"

The first thing that came into Peter's mind was mutiny.

But they had all been there, lined up, all of them. "Who?" he asked.

"The boatswain's mate, Mitchell."

Peter sighed wearily. "He's over there." He pointed to Mitch who was still aboard the 119 helping tie her up alongside *Slewfoot*. "Nobody goes AWOL out here. Where could they go? It's all nothing but jungle."

Mitch, over on the other boat, turned to the 119 bosun and whispered, "I'll swap boats with you, Mac. Over there, no work, lots of sack time, good pay. Best chow in the Navy. Plenty of travel to exotic foreign lands."

"Let me tell you something, Mac," the other bosun said, "I don't even want to be in the same ocean with your boat, much less serve on her." Then he put an arm around Mitch's shoulders. "I feel for you, Mac. But I just can't reach you."

On his way to the captain's cabin Peter found an old rag and wiped the rain off his face and head. He went in first, into Jonesy's cabin, and the first thing he saw was the silver frame with Jonesy's parents smiling so proudly. He laid it face down on the desk and turned to Archer. Peter was determined now to hold his temper. It was important to the boat that he did, because this man had a lot to learn and not much time to learn it in.

"I'm sorry, Adrian," he said. "Really. It was a little rough out the other night."

"I had a rough night, too," Archer told him. "Eighteen hours in the bucket seat of a DC-6, but that hasn't brought me to the point of insubordination."

Peter could feel it burning inside him like a slow fire. Eighteen hours in a plane. Well . . . think of that. All the way from the States. So he kept his mouth shut.

"This is the most undisciplined group of men I ever saw," Archer went on. "As Executive Officer, I want your help in making a taut ship. A taut ship is a happy ship."

Peter wondered whether any of the flames of his anger were

shooting out of his ears. A taut ship is a happy ship. For the love of Mike, get off it!

"They've been out here a long time," Peter said slowly. "A lot of patrols, a lot of fights. They're way past caring whether the ship is taut or whether it's happy. All they want is to fight *Slewfoot* so well they'll stay alive."

"Fight what?" Archer asked.

"That's her name. *Slewfoot*."

"I think from now on we'll call her by her number, Mr. Brent."

Don't get mad, Peter told himself. Just . . . don't . . . get . . . mad. "Call her what you like," he said. "I've got a few names for her myself when those engines won't run and you need 'em."

"Coming back to this matter of discipline. I understand you don't hold quarters every morning."

"Most mornings we've just come back from an all-night patrol."

"It only takes a few minutes to hold quarters, and the backbone of discipline is routine."

Peter opened his fists by rubbing his palms together. Then he said, slowly and keeping his voice low, "This is the only boat in this squadron that has ever made a torpedo run all by herself on three enemy destroyers and sank one of them and got home. That's what I call discipline, not lining up a bunch of men who've been fighting all night just to make an entry in the log that you held quarters."

"I see that you and I have got some problems to work out," Archer said. "I hope we can do it, Mr. Brent."

"I hope so, too," Peter said. "Because if we don't somebody's going to get hurt."

"What do you mean by that?"

Now, Peter thought, if I can just say it quietly and without belting this jerk it might do some good. But he didn't start out very well: "Listen, fella, until your orders are signed by the squadron commander you're not commanding officer of this—*boat*. So let me tell you something before he makes it official.

"*Slewfoot* is the best boat in this war and those are the best men in the Navy and you have been sent out here to replace a man named Jones who had more guts than you and I will ever have. Now I went to the same school you did and learned all about the Navy, but I've been out here awhile and have found out that this isn't the Navy—this is *Slewfoot*, a beat-up mess of plywood which takes all the crew's got just to get her where she's supposed to go, then fight her and bring her back. With nothing left over, Mr. Archer, for quarters and white dress uniforms and discipline. So if you'll excuse me I'll get our spare parts aboard."

Archer handed him a piece of paper, saying, "As you can see, the squadron commander has already signed my orders and I *am* commanding officer of this ship.

"I also understand," Archer went on, "that the rest of the Navy, going by regulations with disciplined crews, is doing quite well in other parts of the world. I think it would be a good idea if this ship joined the rest of the Navy."

This man, Peter thought, is hopeless. At least, right now he is. Maybe after a few patrols . . . a few of those long, long nights.

Peter held out his hand. "Welcome aboard, Adrian."

Archer shook hands briefly and said, "Thank you, Mr. Brent."

Up on Snob Hill, Murph, now back in his tattered dungaree shorts and a ruined T-shirt with Vassar printed across the front, tramped through the mud from his tent to the one Sko and Mitch lived in. They were wandering around, wondering where they could hang up their whites so they would dry.

"So what are we going to do?" Murph demanded.

"Well, there'll come this big wave, see?" Mitch said. "And

somebody will be swept overboard. The night will be real dark, see. So we hunt around but we can't find him."

Sko turned around and looked at them. "And you two swabbies will spend the rest of your lives pounding rocks in the Portsmouth Naval Prison. The guy's new—all he knows is the book. Peter'll get him squared away after a couple of patrols."

Goldberg came in yelling, "At-ten*shun!*"

They turned and looked at him in disgust. Goldberg drew himself up until his head was against the wet tent top. "I want some discipline around here. *Hup*—two—three—four."

"Hup! Your ditty box," Murph said, then turned back to Sko. "I'm not riding a boat with him."

"Oh, get off it, Murph," Sko said. "Let the guy parade around if he wants to. At sea, Peter'll run the boat and dear Adrian can sit in the Skipper's Chair and look at the pretty stars."

Sam, who had come in behind Goldberg, said, "He don't sit in that chair."

"You talk like you own it," Murph said.

Sam looked at them one by one and decided that it was time they knew. "I do," he said.

"So you're the one," Goldberg said.

"That's right. I stole that chair from the Australian Navy. I whipped six of them Aussies for that chair, and so nobody sits in it unless I give 'em permission."

"Well . . ." Goldberg said, "you light-fingered rascal." He went over to Sam and put his arm around him. "Listen, Sam, boy," he whispered, "I know a place stacked with beer. With my influence and your talents we can clean it *out*."

"Come on, you guys," Sko said, "we're holding up the One Nineteen."

They trooped out into the mud, to be joined by the rest of the crew coming out of their tents. Together they griped all the way to the boat, but as soon as they saw Peter and Archer on the deck they went silent and marched aboard, not looking at their new commanding officer.

Sam went directly to the bridge and picked up the chair, which was still lying where it had been thrown by the sweeping water. He folded it carefully and took it below.

7

After a week *Slewfoot* had been patched up and made lethal and was ready for sea again, but, Peter thought, the crew was not.

Sometimes Peter thought that Adrian Archer was not human, that he was some sort of machine. He even talked like a machine, the words coming out as though being typed on a piece of paper. That was bad enough, but he treated the men as though they were machines too—things without feelings, objects to be used regardless of their comfort or welfare.

He didn't "ride" the men, or hard-nose them with personal attacks; he never raised his voice or showed any signs of . . . *anything*. No anger, no pleasure, no praise, no sympathy, no concern. For the first time the thick, dull book of Regulations Governing the United States Navy was broken out and constantly quoted to the laboring men.

Take the matter of the rubber boat.

In the middle of that mean week, the Army had come and asked Peter to pilot their assault boat up to Vadang Island. The Army was as sure as he was that there were no enemy troops on Vadang, but, to play it safe, they wanted to put a twelve-man reconnaissance party ashore.

They were so sure, in fact, that there would be no resistance that they sailed up there in the broad daylight.

And got pasted.

Vadang was *loaded*. As the landing craft nosed in toward a little area of beach and they were on the point of letting the ramp down, they were suddenly bombarded with big and little machine guns, mortar shells splashed all around them and, in a moment, three or four concealed shore battery guns opened up on them.

As the slow and awkward boat maneuvered its way out of there, Peter yearned for the speed and handling of a PT boat. On the other hand, the side armor of the landing craft protected the men crouching behind it, and they got away without any injuries.

"Holy smoke!" the Army captain said. "It's a good thing you had a hole in that rubber boat that night. If you hadn't, you'd have been massacred."

Peter got back to *Slewfoot* late that afternoon and found Mr. Archer on the foredeck. Unfolded in front of him was the rubber boat with the shell holes in it.

"I understand that this boat has been in this condition for some time," he said.

"Thank the Lord," Peter said. "If it hadn't, Murph and I would have been dead pigeons." He turned to Murphy. "Vadang is lousy with guns. We almost got our ears knocked off."

"Yeah?" Murph looked a little scared. "Ambush, eh?"

"You know it," Peter told him. "Just sitting there in the jungle, waiting. Remember to swing wide of Vadang from now on, Murph. They've got some big stuff in there."

"I was speaking of the condition of this rubber boat," Archer said. "I don't understand how an officer with any concern for his men could go to sea with a lifeboat in this condition."

"That's just an extra, Adrian," Peter told him. "The balsa raft is okay and big enough to float us all if she goes down. Anyway, Mitch and I talked the man out of a new one when we were down in Milne."

"Who?" Archer asked.

"Mitch."

"Mitchell, the bosun?"

Peter suddenly got the message, but there was more to come. That night Archer came to his tent and after some discussion about the lack of emergency rations aboard *Slewfoot*,

Archer said, "This matter of first names, Brent. I don't object to your calling me Adrian unofficially, but I prefer that you don't do it in front of the men. I also prefer that you do not call the men by their first names at any time. It breaks down the disciplinary relationship between officer and man."

"Oh, for the love of Mike, Adrian," Peter said. "That stuff is for big ships where you hardly know the men. These guys are like my brothers. Sko wouldn't know who I was talking to if I called him Skowalskilatovich or whatever it is."

"You can do as you wish informally, but it is my preference that you call the men only by their last names aboard ship."

Peter picked his feet up out of the mud and rested them on a log. Then he looked at Archer. The hard, white light of the Coleman gas lamp was full on Archer's face and Peter searched it for some sign of humanness and found none.

There's going to come a time, Peter thought. A time when this man and I are going to have to tangle. And maybe right now is the time. Then he decided against it. A few patrols . . . a few rough nights.

So when finally *Slewfoot* put to sea again it turned out to be a *very* rough night.

The first thing that happened was the Skipper's Chair. Unlike Jonesy and most of the other skippers on the PTs, Archer took the wheel instead of letting the exec or the quartermaster handle it. Peter stood on the bridge with him as they left the Morobe and headed northwest for the Vitiaz Strait.

It was a bad night for PT boats, with a full, warm, close moon, no rain, no clouds. But no wind either, so the sea was calm and *Slewfoot* could, if she needed to, use all the speed she had.

Peter pointed out the landmarks as they went along: Salamaua, Lae, Finschafen, Walingai, and then Umboi Island dark off the starboard side with Long Island ahead. In the dark jungle of New Guinea they could see the occasional flashes of gunfire as the Army moved steadily against the enemy and, on the beaches, they could see the wrecked hulks of ships which had washed ashore there after an encounter with a PT boat at sea.

They gave Vadang Island a wide berth, going to windward of it, and then nosed in again toward the coast.

"Don't put too much faith in the charts," Peter warned him as Archer kept nosing the boat in toward shore. "They're pretty sketchy."

"I've handled boats before," Archer told him.

Peter started to say, "Yeah, but never in these waters," but he stopped himself and just stood there.

After a while Sam came over and tapped Peter on the shoulder. "Your chair's ready, Peter," Sam said.

Peter turned and looked aft. The chair was in its accustomed place but, as he looked at it in the moonlight, something seemed different about it and, for a while, he couldn't tell what it was.

Then he saw it. The QUEEN MARY that had been stenciled on the back canvas was gone.

Peter went over to the chair and looked again. Where QUEEN MARY had been, it now said PETER BRENT, and below that, in smaller letters, was added *Private Property.*

He sat down in the chair and looked at Archer's back. He knew he couldn't ask Sam to change it—Peter had known all along who had swiped the chair—and he also knew that it was going to cause trouble.

The men were settling down now. Jason curled up below his guns with the brand-new barrels; Goldberg and Britches sat together near their rack talking about their home towns; the Preacher was lying stretched out on his two torpedoes trying to read the Bible in the moonlight.

Sko left the engines to the Professor and Skeeter and came on deck, going aft to join Mitch and Stucky. The three of them sat down on the depth charges and talked, knowing that they could not be heard by people on the bridge.

"We got to do something, Sko," Mitch said seriously, "before Mr. Archer gets us all killed. I can't take much more of him."

"Let's get the boys separated from the men," Sko told him. "Let him ride a few patrols and get all that shine off him. Then we'll know what we've really got."

"What we ought to do," Stucky said, "is for all of us to write a letter—you know, like a petition—and everybody sign it and give it to Peter. He can take it to the squadron commander."

"Yeah!" Mitch agreed. "Just lay it on the line. Like breaking us out in the rain for colors. Like standing us up in ranks all the time. Like these field days and inspections and wearing a full uniform. We got a war to fight."

"All those things are in the book," Sko reminded him. "Archer hasn't done a thing that isn't in the book. Anyway, that would just get Peter into more trouble than he's already in. No. All we can do is wait and see if Archer doesn't get with it."

"Peter's the one taking the real beating," Stucky said. "I don't see how he keeps from letting Archer have it."

"Where it won't blind him," Mitch said.

Murph came out of the chart house and looked around. Then he went over to the pelorus and took a look. He started to say something to Archer, changed his mind and went over to Peter in the chair. "Aren't we pretty close to where the One Twenty hit that coral?" he whispered.

"About five miles."

"I better tell him," Murph said.

"Wait. If he doesn't ease off in a minute or so, I'll tell him."

Archer did not, however, change course. Peter got up out of the chair and went to stand beside Archer on the platform. For a moment he stood in silence watching the dark coast off the port side, picking out the landmarks easily in the moonlight. With rather elaborate concern he took a few bearings. All this had no effect on Archer, who held the boat on course.

Finally Peter decided that he had better forget the regulations about telling the commanding officer what to do. "There's a coral reef dead ahead," he said. "It's not marked on the charts but it's there. The One Twenty hit it the other night."

"I discussed that with the captain of the One Twenty. It is now marked on my chart. I'm well clear of it."

Peter didn't think so, but as he started to object, Archer said, "Is this the fashion in which you allow the men to behave at general quarters, Mr. Brent?"

"They'll get to those guns quick enough if anything happens, Adrian. The nights get pretty long out here and it's better to have them rested and ready."

Archer turned and looked at him for a moment and then he leaned forward and called out, "All hands! Man your battle stations!"

The dark figures of the men jumped instantly to guns and torpedo racks and cannon. Murph came tearing out of the shack, looking wildly around for the enemy. Willie, the radarman, searched the empty scope and then poked his head out of the hatch and looked around.

Goldberg came over below the bridge and said, "What's up, Captain?"

"When this boat is on patrol," Archer said, "all hands will man their battle stations at all times. And, Goldberg, there will be no talking."

Goldberg stared up at him, his face suddenly sullen in the moonlight, then, in silence, he turned away.

"Goldberg," Archer called to him.

Goldberg turned around again.

"That was an order I gave you. How do you acknowledge an order?"

Goldberg looked big and menacing as he walked slowly back to the bridge. He said the right words, but he could have been court-martialed for the way he said them. "Aye, aye . . . sir," Goldberg said. Then he stood there, looking up at Archer as though daring him to open his mouth again. Finally Goldberg turned away, walked forward and bawled out, "Okay, you guys, the commanding officer of this 'ship' says for you to stand up on your feet at your battle stations and there will be no talking."

Peter was watching Archer, and now for the first time he saw a small sign of satisfaction in Archer's expression.

And then the satisfaction disappeared as Goldberg added loudly, "And if standing up all night makes you too pooped to pull the trigger, report to me."

Archer turned to Peter. "I think it's time we had an example, Mr. Brent. Have Goldberg report to captain's mast tomorrow afternoon."

"What's he done?" Peter asked. "What are you going to charge him with?"

"It is part of the duties of the executive officer to prefer charges against the men," Archer said.

Peter looked at him in the moonlight. The time was coming, he thought, and it was coming fast. "Okay," Peter said. "As Executive Officer I find nothing in Goldberg's conduct to warrant bringing him to mast."

Behind them someone snickered . . . out loud. Peter and Archer turned around to see who it was.

Peter had never seen Murph so busy, so concentrated. The protractor and parallel rulers were flying around on the chart.

"What do you find so funny, Murphy?" Archer asked.

Murph looked up with an innocent Irish face. "I guess I must've been thinking about when I had a hot rod, Mr. Archer. That thing could *travel* and this night I had this chick, see, and she said 'Drive *slow*, darling . . . so we can talk.' And, you know, I fell for it."

Archer, apparently satisfied turned back to the wheel, but

Peter stood looking sternly at Murph. Suddenly all the innocence vanished as Murph winked at him and grinned.
Peter had to turn away to keep from laughing out loud.

Willie poked his head up then and said, "We're getting in
pretty close, Mr. Brent."

"Okay," Peter acknowledged and turned to Archer. "Want
to give her a little sea room, Cap'n?"

Archer, without turning his head, said, "The element of
surprise can be gained for the PT boat by staying close to the
shore and thus confusing the image of the enemy's radar."

Right out of the mouth of the professor in the school at
Melville, Rhode Island—a long way from New Guinea in the
Pacific Ocean.

"With a full-moon tide you get a pretty strong set toward
shore around here," Peter said. "You make more leeway
than you figure sometimes."

"When Mr. Jones was commanding officer was it your
custom to tell him how to handle the ship, Mr. Brent?"

Well, you long drink of water, Peter thought. "No," he
said quietly, "it wasn't. Because Jonesy never held the boat
on a course that would put a coral head through her hull."

"And you think I am?"

"I don't *think* so. I know it," Peter told him.

The engines were rolling at 900 rpm, the boat sliding
along, bow down, at about 12 knots.

If she had been going fast enough to lift the bow it would
have taken the bottom out of her when she hit, bows on.

Even at 12 knots *Slewfoot* hit hard. For a moment her bow
crunched through the outer layer of living, soft coral, but
then it struck the rock-hard structure of the long-dead coral,
which stopped her dead in her wake.

It threw Goldberg back against Britches, and the two of
them stumbled in a weird, awkward dance back against the
bridge structure. The sudden stop peeled the Preacher off the
torpedoes and rolled him aft until he hit the legs of Goldberg
and Britches and brought them down on top of him. It

bruised Jason against the gun mount and flung Willie almost head on against the radarscope. It tumbled Stucky and Mitch over the depth charges so that when the moving wake struck the stern and climbed over it, they were rolled back against the launcher.

In the engine room, Sko didn't wait for the buzzer but yanked the engines out of gear, while on the bridge, Peter instantly hauled the throttles back.

Then it was very quiet on *Slewfoot*. Still and quiet, only the low panting of the muffled, idling engines and the wash of water against the coral made noise.

8

Archer was the first to speak, and he said it as though discussing the weather in Des Moines, Iowa. "I must have been misinformed by the captain of the One Twenty boat."

"Something like that," Peter told him.

"We'll back her off," Archer said, reaching for the buzzer and throttles.

"Don't you think we'd better find out if she's hurt first?" Peter asked.

"I should have thought you would already be on your way below," Archer said.

"Okay, so don't back her until I find out."

As he turned to go below, Sam the cook came charging out of the hatch, yelling, "Water's coming in the boat!"

"Okay, Sam," Peter said. "Let's have a look."

As he went down the hatch he could hear Archer snapping out orders. "Stand by the life rafts! All hands check your life jackets!" Then he turned to Murphy and snapped, "Get out all confidential charts and codes. Secure them in the sea disposal pouch. Be sure the lead weights are in it."

Peter dropped down through the hatch and as he followed Sam forward he marveled at Archer. He was barking orders exactly as it said in the book, in exactly the right words, and if he didn't stop pretty soon he'd get to the place where the book said abandon ship and they'd all jump overboard before Archer even found out what sort of trouble *Slewfoot* was in.

She was in plenty of trouble. It made Peter sick to see it and outraged him because it was so unnecessary.

In the port bow, about a foot above the dayroom deck, a jagged, half-crushed piece of coral had rammed its way through the thin plywood hull and was sticking into the compartment. Water was pouring in around it and running aft along the slightly up-slanted deck.

Peter was looking at it, figuring what to do about it, when he felt the engines begin to turn up and then felt *Slewfoot* begin to shiver and then to groan and strain and shake. Peter could hear outside the boat the rush of the water along the hull as the screws backed with all the power of the three Packards.

The force of the engines was ripping a larger hole in her, the coral not moving, but the plywood hull steadily tearing away.

Peter snapped at Sam, "Tell him to stop going astern. Tell Mitch to get down here with a sledgehammer and chisel."

As Sam ran for the hatch, Peter went aft to the engine room and told the Professor to start all pumps and keep 'em going. Then he went up the amidships hatch and stuck his head out. As he did, Archer stalked over to him and stood above him. There was still no anger in the man— *nothing*. "Did you send an enlisted man to give me orders, Mr. Brent?"

Peter said it before he even knew the words were coming out. "Stop backing the boat, you idiot! You're tearing it apart!"

Archer just stood there, looking down at him. "Is that your idea of a damage report, Mr. Brent?"

Peter let his wrath subside a little and said, "A piece of coral has holed her forward and she isn't coming off until we get that coral out of her. She's going to take a lot of water, but I think the pumps can handle it."

"I'll inspect the damage myself," Archer said. Then he turned to Murphy. "See that my orders are carried out, quartermaster."

Murph looked startled. "About the rafts?"

"Exactly," Archer said, and came below with Peter.

They went forward to find Mitch and Sko banging away at the coral with a big ripping chisel and a sledgehammer. "Belay that!" Archer snapped at them. "Who gave you orders to cut that away?"

Sko looked helplessly at Peter. "I did," Peter said.

Archer only glanced at him and then went to the coral. With his hands he measured the hole it had made and then stood for a moment, watching the water flowing in around the coral.

Walking on tiptoe so as not to get his shoes any wetter than necessary, Archer crossed the room and sat down on one of the bunks, his feet up out of the water. Then he took out a notebook and pencil and began some sort of figuring while Sko, Mitch and Peter watched him. When he got through figuring he said, "If that obstruction is cleared from the breach in the hull, the capacity of the bilge pumps will not be as great as the capacity of the area through which the sea can enter."

"Then we'll bail her with the fire buckets," Peter told him.

Archer got off the bunk and waded aft. At the door he motioned for Peter to follow him.

"Get some caulking around that thing," Peter told Mitch. "Keep as much water out as you can." Then he followed Archer into the captain's cabin. Archer carefully closed the door and then sat down at the little desk. After he got through wiping the water off his shoes he looked up at Peter.

"It's very bad for discipline to reprimand a junior officer

in front of members of the crew," Archer said calmly. "You realize now, don't you, that if they had carried out your orders and cut away that coral and the boat had been backed off into deep water she would have sunk?"

Peter was so amazed he couldn't say anything. He just stood there looking at the guy.

"Now," Archer went on, still in that perfectly calm way, "we have three alternatives. First, we can build a cofferdam around the breach in the hull, then remove the coral—from the outside, Mr. Brent. Secondly, we can stay where we are— the pumps are now able to handle the water coming in around that coral—until daylight. The Army patrol planes will spot us then and send help. Thirdly, we can abandon ship now and row the rafts southeast along the coast until we reach an area held by the Army."

The wave of anger went all over Peter again but this time he managed to control it and tried to make his own voice sound as flatly calm as that of Archer.

"We have *no* alternatives, Mr. Archer. By the time we could build a cofferdam with the tools we've got, it would be daylight. If we abandon ship and try to row those rafts, the set of the tide—it's rising, you know—would put us ashore within a mile, and the Army is nowhere near here yet."

It didn't seem to be making any impression on Archer, and suddenly Peter understood why. In the school in Melville, Rhode Island, Peter remembered, there had been a great deal of instruction about how to handle the boats and to keep them running, and how to be a leader of men; a great deal of training with the guns and torpedoes, and a lot of what they called strategy and tactics, station keeping, and navigation. But they hadn't taught much about the way things were in the South Pacific.

"As soon as it's daylight," Peter said, telling him quietly about how things really are in the South Pacific, "they'll open up on us. It'll take those shore batteries of theirs about five minutes to cut this boat up into kindling wood.

"Or," Peter went on, "they might wait a little while. They might wait to see what came to help us and then open up."

"You confirm my first decision," Archer said. "We will wait until the tide changes. Then we can row the rafts down the coast to Army territory. The Japanese certainly wouldn't fire on helpless men in life rafts."

Peter stared at him, not believing, and then said quietly, "Adrian, you aren't in the Ivy League now."

Peter started to tell him how personal the war was with the men in PT boats—personal and bitter, with no quarter asked or given—but decided not to. Archer would just have to find that out for himself.

"The only thing is to get this boat away from here," Peter told him. "Now, while it's dark. Once we get her off and under way, I think Sko can get enough out of the engines to keep her going bow high so we'll only ship the tops of waves."

Archer didn't seem to be listening. He looked up at Peter slowly and said, "Would they shoot helpless men in a life raft?"

"They have," Peter said. "So let's get out of here."

Archer made no move to get up, but he nodded and that was all Peter needed.

He went back into the dayroom and told Mitch and Sko to cut away the coral. Then he went on topside to talk to Goldberg and the Preacher.

"We may have to dump these fish," he told them, "so disarm them. I don't want to get blown off this reef."

"Wow!" Goldberg said. "Fifty thousand dollars worth of the poor taxpayers' money over the side."

"Remember that sign," Peter said. "'It takes millions to win a war, but all you've got to lose one.' Get the racks flipped over as soon as you disarm, and when I give the word, let 'em go."

He went below again and helped Mitch and Sko with the coral.

They were lucky. As the chisel cut down through it, the

coral suddenly broke, the crack running outside the boat and slanting forward so that, if she moved aft, the remaining coral would slide past her.

Water now came in in a solid rushing column. Peter yelled up the hatch, "Back her down. All hands on the fire buckets."

Then, on the ladder, he looked back a moment at the water, now coming up toward Mitch's knees.

Going on deck, Peter waited for the feel of the engines turning up and the feel of the boat straining. Nothing happened.

He ran aft to the bridge.

There was no one there. He looked around for Archer, then, not finding him, buzzed for astern and eased the throttles forward.

Slewfoot groaned, shivered and finally shook wildly, but she did not move astern.

"Let the fish go," Peter called down and eased the throttles ahead again.

That did it. With the deadweight of the torpedoes off her, *Slewfoot* broke loose from the bed of coral and slid backward into deeper water.

Forward, the men were passing the fire buckets up through the hatch and dumping them over the side.

As soon as he had room to turn her, Peter buzzed for ahead and eased her around, pointing her toward the open sea.

The fire buckets weren't doing much good. As Peter swung the wheel over, *Slewfoot* responded like a truck, the water lying heavy in her belly; but she came slowly around and as soon as she was clear, he rammed the throttles all the way to the stops and prayed that she would lift a little— lift enough to get that hole in her bow above the solid water.

All hands except the engine-room gang were on the fire buckets, so Peter had to yell at them to move aft to add their weight to that of the engines and get her stern down.

As the men streamed aft in the darkness Peter felt the

boat rising, the bow coming up above the horizon. He also felt a great sluggish tide of water rolling aft through the boat. He ran back to the hatch and yelled down, "Dog the engine-room door."

But Sko was way ahead of him. The onrushing water hit the already closed door and stopped. The bucket brigade moved up enough to start bailing her from the amidships hatch, and the bow slowly rose higher and higher.

They bailed her all the way back to the Morobe River, all the time knowing that they'd never get her home.

Along the banks of the Morobe were the tents and build-ings, supply dumps and motor pools, guns and ammunition, foods, medicines—everything for a war. Peter knew that he could not, for only the sake of *Slewfoot*, take her at speed up the river. Those Packards made a wake like a tidal wave, which, if he tried to ram her home, would wash up over the low, muddy banks, flood the living and supply areas and ruin, with muddy water, millions of dollars worth of equip-ment.

Peter also knew that as soon as he slowed her down her bow would drop, the hole in it would slide under water, and then the river would come into her far faster than the pumps and the exhausted men could bail it out. They might make it to her rickety dock, but even if they did, *Slewfoot* would inevitably sink. In his mind Peter could see Sko's face as that filthy water rushed into his engine room and poured over those Packards.

"Pick us out a nice mudbank, Murph," he said, as he turned her from the open sea toward the mouth of the river.

"How about that one at six buoy?"

"Very fine," Peter agreed. "Tell all hands to get set. We're going to hit pretty hard."

He would never forget it. Still at speed, he turned her bows toward the mudbank with the crawling jungle just behind. At the first faint slither of mud against her, he yanked the throttles back and gave Sko a frantic buzz to take her out of gear.

For a long moment it looked as though *Slewfoot* was going to slide across the mud into the interior of New Guinea. The solid mass of the jungle rushed at her as Sko cut the engines altogether, leaving the boat silent as she ploughed up on the mudbank and finally came to rest, her bows neatly between two palm trees, her hull almost entirely out of the water.

The men got slowly to their feet and looked around. There was nothing to say. They just stood there looking at their boat stuck in the mud while the frightened land crabs regained their courage and cautiously came out of the darkness to investigate her, their big ugly bodies rattling against her bow.

Behind him Peter heard Archer's calm voice, "Well done, Mr. Brent. Post a four-man watch and dismiss the crew."

"What do we need a watch for?" Peter asked. "Let everybody get some sleep and some chow and we'll strike a blow for liberty tomorrow."

"A four-man watch," Archer said. Then he hopped down off the bridge, walked over to the side and jumped down into the mud. The men watched in silence as he slogged, knee-deep in mud, up to the jungle and disappeared.

"Gerry," Peter said, "you and Britches take the first watch. Preacher, you and Murph take the other. The rest of you get some rest."

"What are we supposed to be 'watching' for?" Goldberg asked.

"Pirates, what else?" Peter said, dropping down through the hatch. As he went forward he heard Goldberg sternly order Britches to go get his broadsword. "We might have to repel boarders," Goldberg told him.

In a moment Jason and Murph came down the forward hatch and joined him in the dayroom. The lower bunks were soaked with water, but the uppers were sleepable.

The three of them examined the hole in her hull. Now that the sea wasn't pouring through it, it didn't look like such a terrible wound. "We'll be back in business in a couple of days," Peter told them.

"Somebody ought to catch a court-martial for this," Murph declared angrily, staring at the ragged plywood with the moonlight streaming through the hole.

"If everybody in PTs got court-martialed for a goof," the Preacher said, "we'd all be in jail."

Peter left them arguing the point and went into the tiny exec's cabin. He stretched out on the bunk with his clothes on and tried to keep his mind on the details of getting the boat repaired and off the mudbank and back in business. But time after time, his mind drifted off to the big thing— Archer.

Sometime during the short night a thought struck him *hard*. Could it be, he wondered, that Archer went by the book because that was all he knew?

And much later, there was a knock at the door. Peter didn't think he had fallen asleep, but he must have, because he dreamed that someone was calling him. He turned on the light and sat up, listening.

Someone whispered outside the door, "Mr. Brent?"

Peter swung his feet around to the deck and said, "Come in."

The little Irishman had an expression of absolute terror as he slipped into the cabin and carefully closed the door. Peter had seen Murph scared a lot of times, but he had never seen him as shaken up as he was now. "What's the trouble, Murph?"

"Bad," Murph said, his voice low. Then, before he went on, he looked back over his shoulder to be sure no one was there. "You know, the Captain told me to put the charts and codes in the pouch with the lead weights so we could sink 'em if we had to."

"No, I didn't," Peter said, surprised.

"Well, he did. Then he told me to put the pouch in the rubber boat when they lowered it overboard."

Peter stiffened, his breath whistling through his teeth. "Where's the boat now?"

"That's what I mean," Murph said, almost crying. "I forgot it. I guess when we went astern it tore loose. It's *gone!*"

It was like being hit in the back of the head with an ax. For a moment Peter could do nothing but stare in horror at Murph. Murph backed away from him until he backed into the door.

"It wasn't all my fault," he wailed.

"It doesn't make any difference whose fault it is," Peter told him. "If the Japs get hold of those codes we're sunk. Does the skipper know about this?"

"I was afraid to tell him. . . . What'll he do to me, Peter?"

"Does anybody else know?"

"I don't think so. Everybody was running all over the place. What'll he do to me?"

Peter wasn't listening to him now as he sat thinking about the code books in the disposal pouch.

Peter knew that the U.S. strategy against the enemy had changed. There weren't going to be any more Guadalcanals where the Marines were put ashore at one end of a grisly island to fight their way, inch by bloody inch, to the other end. From now on U.S. forces were going to leapfrog their way through the Pacific, leapfrog up New Guinea. With short, smashing amphibious attacks they were going to take and hold only enough area to use as a base for the next hop. They were going to take Salamaua and then Lae, Finschafen and then Wewak and Hollandia.

But these places were not called by their names. Each had a code name of its own—like Sunrise and Rosarita and Pittsburgh. These names were in the pouch now adrift somewhere in enemy waters. Let them find it and the entire top-secret code of the operation could be broken and every message that had been sent in code could be read.

"What'll he do to me?" Murph wailed.

"Right now that's not important," Peter said, as he started rolling up his pants legs. "I want you to disappear, Murph, so he can't ask you—if he happens to think about it. Go up to Six Squadron and stay there until I send for you. And don't say a word to anyone about this. Understand?"

"Yes, sir," Murphy said, terrified.

"Okay, get going," Peter said.

When Murphy had gone, Peter sat there on the bed for a little while longer, thinking through this problem.

And when he came to the end of it he found himself faced with a dreadful decision.

Now, Peter knew, it was in his power to rid *Slewfoot* of Adrian Archer forever. All he had to do was go to the squadron commander and report this thing and Archer would be hauled up for a general court-martial and that would be the end of him as far as *Slewfoot* was concerned. It would also wipe out Murph, Peter knew.

But what about the other twelve men whose lives were absolutely dependent on the life of *Slewfoot*?

In the silent boat, with the night so close around him, Peter was convinced that if Adrian Archer stayed as skipper he would kill them all. And kill the boat.

9

Peter Brent despised airplanes because, secretly, he was afraid of them. He wouldn't admit this to himself, arguing that nothing was so important in life you had to get up in the air and fly real fast to get somewhere. To him, airplanes were dangerous, untrustworthy machines designed to kill you. They were not at all like boats that were friendly and had as much desire to live as you did. Peter couldn't imagine any man having any sort of affection for an airplane. Airplanes were enemies.

But, as he rode along in the Army jeep, looking at the airplanes lined up on the hardstands, he resigned himself to having to fly in one. It was the only way to find that yellow rubber boat with, he hoped, the pouch and the codes still in it.

As the sun came up bright and hot in a cloudless sky, he picked out the airplane that, since he had to, he wanted to ride in. It was one of the new, fast fighters. Low and sleek and, he had to admit, powerful looking, with a feeling that it was going fast just standing there in the sunshine.

But the jeep driver drove on past all of the fighters, past the bombers, past *everything*.

Peter never felt really comfortable around the Army and this driver made him particularly uncomfortable, acting as though Peter were asking him to sacrifice his life or something. As they passed the last of the parked airplanes and roared on down the empty and deserted runway, Peter got up enough courage to say, "I'm supposed to get in one of those planes."

"That's right," the driver said, gunning the jeep even faster.

"I think the pilot's waiting," Peter said.

"Pilots," the driver said with disgust.

"I mean," Peter said, "do you know where you're going?"

The driver turned and looked at him for a long, cold moment but didn't say anything.

Then suddenly and so fast it almost flung Peter out of the jeep, he wheeled the thing off the runway, crashed across a strip of rough ground and braked to a sliding stop near a clump of trees.

"End of the line," the driver said.

Peter looked around but could see nothing but the end of the runway with the jungle all around it. "Where's my plane?" he asked.

"In there somewhere," the driver said, pointing toward the jungle. Then he nervously gunned the motor as a signal for Peter to get out and leave him alone. Peter got out.

The jeep took off with all four wheels spinning, slammed back to the runway and disappeared.

Peter walked cautiously into the sparse jungle and found the airplane.

It was *tiny*. A little high-wing monoplane with a little coffee-grinder engine up front and a propeller not much longer than Peter's arms. It was streaked with mud, a sad vine was dripping off one wing, and one of the cockpit doors was flapping sadly back and forth in the morning wind.

Peter, feeling the same cold sickness he often felt just before a fight in *Slewfoot*, walked slowly over to the plane. There was no one in the little cockpit—or anywhere else.

There were two beat-up metal seats, side-by-side. In each there was a brown, thin, ragged canvas cushion, the stuffing pooching out of a slit in one of them. On the mud-covered floor about two million ants were eating what was left of a Spam sandwich. Hanging from the radio tuning knob was a little hula girl made out of pink rubber. She was swinging back and forth in the wind. Sticking out of the map compartment under the dash were two or three well-read comic books, but no maps.

"You Ensign Brent?" a voice asked from behind him.

The man was an apparition. He hadn't had a haircut in nine months, and long stalks of it hung down over his face so he looked like he was peering through some sort of a fence. Then, when that hair stopped just below his nose, an enormous moustache took up. Every hair in the moustache was going in a different direction and to Peter it looked like a tangle of barbed wire. The only clothing he had on was a pair of ragged, paint-stained shorts. No shoes, no shirt, no hat. He was lean, muscular and tan.

"Yeah," Peter said.

"I'm Lieutenant Carruthers, your pilot, sir. Where you want to go?"

"Up the coast through the Vitiaz," Peter said, shaking hands.

"Hop in," Carruthers said.

"In *this?*" Peter asked, backing away from it.

"What else?"

Carruthers stooped under the wing and went to the sad, flapping door. He took it off and laid it on the ground. Then he went around to the other side and took that door off too.

"They just get in the way in case you have to jump out," he said.

Peter wasn't *about* to get into this wreck. "Er . . . your Operations people said something about an L-85. You know, something with a little more . . . well . . . er . . ."

Carruthers climbed into the cockpit, saying, "Meet the L-85. Her name's Deborah." Then he sat there, looking expectantly at Peter.

There was nothing for it but to get in. If this had been the Navy, Peter wouldn't have minded saying that he wasn't going to get into any such contraption as this, but with the Army . . .

As he sat down on the slit cushion, he noticed the vine hanging off the wing. "'Want me to pull that vine off?" he asked hopefully.

"It'll either blow off or we'll take it along and drop it on the Japs."

Peter squirmed around in the seat, looking behind and under it for the parachute harness. He could find nothing that even faintly resembled a parachute. "How do you hook up the chute?" he asked.

"Chute?" the pilot asked, sounding surprised. "Listen, you ever sit on a parachute pack for a couple of hours? Like sitting on a pile of rocks."

"I won't mind," Peter assured him.

"Maybe not," he said, "but it doesn't make any difference because there aren't any."

"What happens if you get hit?" Peter asked, his voice sounding weak and faraway.

"Ride her down," Carruthers said. "She floats like a chute anyhow."

It made Peter sick and all he could do, as the engine began to make dreadful coughing noises, was sit there and stare straight ahead.

The engine suddenly stopped coughing and panting and began to run, and when it did it seemed to Peter that the plane was going to fall apart. The wings waggled around drunkenly and the whole plane shook and rattled. The engine, with no cowling around it, bounced around just in front of him until Peter wondered if it was attached to the plane. Clouds of blue smoke poured out of it and were swept into the cockpit by the whirling propeller. And then, when the smoke died down a little, Peter looked with horror at long, hot flames shooting out of both sides of the engine.

He glanced over at the lieutenant, expecting him to cut the engine immediately and—Peter prayed—report this thing as absolutely unflyable; but the lieutenant just shoved the throttle all the way forward, took his feet off the brakes and away they went, staggering and wobbling out from under the trees, bouncing savagely across the strip and finally hitting the end of the runway. There it rolled along, the wings wobbling up and down, the vine still streaming from one of them.

By some miracle the plane rose into the air. Peter looked out with horror and saw the ground dropping away below him. Surely, he thought, as the engine streamed blue flame, this pilot would put it down on the ground again and run away.

The pilot was paying no attention to the plane. He wasn't even looking out of it, but was bent over, searching around for something on the floor.

He found the ant-covered piece of sandwich and picked it up. As he flung it out of the plane he said, "I never saw as many ants as they've got out here."

"Lots of ants," Peter said, his mouth dry as sandpaper. "Don't you even have seat belts?"

"There's one around someplace."

Peter, after a long search, found the belt tangled up under the seat. He untangled it and strapped it on. "You don't use a seat belt?" he asked.

"Not until they shoot at me. I got sort of a nervous stomach," the pilot said, taking his left foot off the pedal and sticking it and half his leg out the door so it waved around in the prop wash. Then he took his other foot off the other pedal and rested it comfortably on the instrument panel.

"The vine's gone," Peter said.

"Too bad. Hey, what are we looking for?"

"A yellow rubber boat."

"Where'd you lose it?"

"Up near Vadang, but on the mainland side of the strait."

"What's the matter? You a supply officer and lost it and they're going to make you pay for it?"

"No. We lost it off a PT boat."

The pilot jerked around in the seat and stared at him through the dripping of lanky hair. His voice sounded awed and frightened as he asked, "Are you a PT-boat man?"

Peter nodded.

The pilot shook his head back and forth. "You know what I'd do if somebody told me I had to ride in one of those PT boats? I'd shoot myself."

Peter was suddenly completely absorbed by a gauge which he could just see past the pilot's dirty bare foot on the instrument panel. The needle of the gauge was up against the pin on the EMPTY side.

"Is that the gas gauge?" he asked.

The pilot nodded and said, "I wouldn't put foot on one of those PT boats if it was in a museum in Milwaukee."

Peter pointed a shaking finger at the gas gauge. "It's reading *empty*," he said.

"It always does," the pilot said, not looking at it. "Man,

it's just suicide riding those boats. What chance have you *got?* They can hit you with a slingshot and all that aviation gas goes up like a bomb."

But Peter's attention was fixed on the instruments. The compass was reading due south but, when he looked out of the plane, they were heading northwest. "Is the compass working?" he asked, his voice falling almost to a whisper.

"If it is, it's the first time," the pilot said. "You must be out of your mind to ride in those boats."

Peter had never felt so lost and helpless in his life, but there was absolutely nothing he could do about it. "Oh, they're not so bad," he said. "At least when they get in trouble they don't fall ten thousand feet and splatter you all over the landscape like this contraption."

"Who's falling?" the pilot asked, a little indignant. "You've only got one place to go in those boats—*down.* I can go anywhere I like and this ain't no 'contraption.'"

"Sorry," Peter said. "But I'll take the boats anytime to one of these whatever you call 'em. A boat's pretty hard to see and pretty hard to hit."

"I lie in my sack at night and listen to you guys going out in those floating plywood bombs and I say 'thank the Lord I'm in the Air Corps,' and then I go to sleep." The pilot began fishing around in the cockpit until he found the ends of the seat belt. Without pulling his leg back into the plane or taking his foot off the instrument panel he buckled the ends around his "nervous stomach" and began to sing.

"Oh, there'll be mushrooms in the sky," he sang in a croaking voice. "Cah-*chung* cah-*chung* cah-*chung.*"

It was bad enough just being in the plane, Peter thought, without this madman for a pilot.

"You ever see mushrooms in the sky?" the pilot asked.

"No."

"You will."

They had crossed the Huon Gulf and Peter expected him to swing to the right and follow the peninsula, but, instead, he kept on a straight course which carried them back over the dark green jungle.

"Mushrooms in the sky," the pilot said. "With rocks in 'em. Cah-*chung*." Then he looked over at Peter. "We're going to get shot down," he said calmly.

Before Peter could answer, the sun suddenly disappeared, the sky turned black and, in the plane, there was a strong, acrid smell of burning gunpowder.

And almost instantly there was a tremendous, earsplitting stomach-jarring, bone-rattling explosion which sounded exactly like "cah-*chung*."

Following that were more and more cah-*chungs* and the plane began to rock violently, thrown this way and that by the bursts of antiaircraft shells all around it.

Peter grabbed for the instrument panel but couldn't reach it as the plane was flung down, ramming him back into the seat.

As it came out of the black roaring smoke Peter saw that it was falling, totally out of control, and spinning as it fell. Above them he could still hear the antiaircraft shells exploding—cha-*chung* cha-*chung* BLAM BLAM BLAM. He tried to look up but couldn't, so looked down.

Below him—far below him—the sea and the jungle were whirling slowly and jerkily around, and as they whirled he whirled too, his body being slammed around in the seat, only the belt keeping him from being thrown out.

He was doomed, Peter decided. Nothing could save him now. The jungle, spinning like a green top, was rushing up toward him. And even the engine had been knocked out, he noticed, as the propeller suddenly appeared, the little blades spinning lazily around and around, driven, he decided, by the wind of their fall.

In the movies, he remembered, in a situation like this our hero always came up with some funny remark that showed how nonchalant and brave he was and Peter felt that it was his duty to say something, but all he could say was, "That's

what I mean about the PT boats. What do we do now?"
"Do?" the pilot asked. "Nothing."

Peter decided that he should have been able to figure that one out for himself. With no parachute he couldn't jump out. And with the plane out of control and powerless there was no way to level off and land—even if there had been some place other than the terrible jungle to land *on*.

The cah-*chungs* were faint and faraway now and it seemed to Peter that the little noises he heard only made everything sound more silent. The wind was whistling eerily around the plane, the engine was making little, pitiful, coughing and panting noises, some gears somewhere were chattering oilily, and from the radio a flat, unexcited voice was talking about the weather.

A man in a PT boat never would feel as helpless and awful as this, Peter decided. In the boats there would always be something you could *do* to try to save your life. You wouldn't have to sit like this, strapped into a seat, with no way in the world to keep this airplane from killing you as it spun on down into the jungle where the tall, hard trees would tear it apart and tear you apart too.

The jungle was so close Peter could see the individual trees sticking up at him like so many deadly and enormous spears. He could even see the fronds of the coconut palms and the vines. And they were *rushing* upward at him, reaching out for him.

In the last seconds of his life, Peter closed his eyes. Why look at it coming? he asked himself.

It felt like a giant had slammed a hand against his chest and rammed him backward. He waited for the sound of the plane being torn apart, the sound of the trees tearing into him, the feel of pain and blood and the last seconds of life.

Nothing else happened. In fact, the engine began to run again.

But when he opened his eyes he saw that they were down in the jungle all right. A giant of a tree was rushing straight

toward them—like a wall of green leaves, and gray, huge
limbs and trunk, and those slimy vines.

How did that tree get into that position? Peter wondered.
They should have been coming straight down toward the top
of it, not slamming into it sideways.

And then the tree seemed to shrink an inch or two and
disappear in a green flash under his feet.

And nothing was spinning around any more.

Peter took a deep breath and looked around. The plane
was flying straight and level just inches above the tops of the
trees, which were flashing under it like a green sea. When
Peter looked back he could see the leaves waving around in
the prop wash and the long vines coiling around like snakes.

"Listen to Tokyo Rose tonight," the pilot said. "You'll
hear all about how we got shot down."

Peter just stared at him as the plane passed over the last
of the land and flew out over the Bismarck Sea.

"I've been shot down that way nineteen times, according
to Tokyo Rose."

"You did that—on purpose?"

"You know how it is," the pilot said, smoothing the wild
hairs of his moustache with his fingers. "Those guys sit down
there in that stinking jungle and seldom get a shot at us.
Why not make 'em feel good? Make 'em feel like they've
shot you down and accomplished something."

"Yeah," Peter said, "I guess you're right. But you know
what I'd like for you to do sometime, ol' buddy . . . go riding
with me on a PT boat."

"Not on your life," the pilot said. "Too dangerous."

10

                                                  Peter was
beginning to get a little more faith in the airplane. Not much,
but a *little.* And a little more faith in this wild man flying it.

But Peter was scheming how to get this Army lieutenant aboard *Slewfoot*. A ride in the boat was what he needed to round out his life.

They were out over the Bismarck Sea now, flying close along the green shore of New Guinea. As Peter looked down at the surface of the sea he wished that he had flown over here before, for now he could see many rocks and shoals and coral reefs he had never seen before. He marveled as he looked at them that *Slewfoot* had lived so long without hitting any of them.

"You know, the closest I ever got to being really shot down," the pilot was saying, "was with a coconut."

If ever a warrior needed a Section Eight for insanity, this was the one, Peter thought, looking at the wind blowing through that moustache and making it wave in all directions.

"I was flying along minding my own business," the pilot went on, "when I jumped over some trees and down into a flat area—a farm or something—and there they were, running for their lives. But one of them stood his ground and threw a coconut at me. Hit me, too. Peeled off the left aileron and almost spun me in. It made me so mad I turned around and bombed him with my last can of Spam. Missed him, though."

"Don't you carry any guns at all?" Peter asked.

"I used to. But some flak bounced me around one day and the gun went off and shot a hole through the radio. Through the roof, too, and when it started to rain it dripped all down the back of my neck. No more guns."

"Whoa!" Peter said suddenly. "That's where we went aground."

Looking at it from a hundred feet up and in the broad daylight he wondered how the 120 boat and then Archer had failed to see the coral reef. It was low tide now and the sea was washing over it, changing suddenly from a bluish green to sparkling white.

"What do we do?" the pilot asked.

Peter looked over at the deep, dark green of the jungle on New Guinea and then over at the thinner, sparser green of the islands. Although he could see no sign of the enemy he knew that many eyes were watching the dirty little plane as it floated along in the clear, sunshiny air. "We'd better not do too much circling around," he said, "or they'll know we're looking for something, and they might start looking too. We hit that reef we just passed. The wind has been steady out of the west so let's turn east and hold a steady course."

"That'll be up to you," the pilot said. "North, south, east and west don't mean a thing to me."

"What would you do if you got lost?"

"Just find a railroad track and fly down it until I got somewhere."

Peter made a resolution not to make a habit of flying in airplanes with this pilot. He pointed to the east and Carruthers swung the little plane around and settled her on course.

"That's Vadang straight ahead," Peter told him. "Swing wide of it. It's loaded."

"That's what I hear," the pilot said. "I also heard that one of those crazy PT-boat men wanted to go ashore on it—all by himself."

"With another guy," Peter corrected him.

"Was that you?" the pilot asked, amazed. "What are you, some sort of hero, or something?"

"No. Just crazy."

They were approaching Vadang, and Peter looked down at it with interest. Even in the bright light of the day he could see absolutely no sign of the enemy, no sign of machine-gun emplacements or revetments for the big guns he knew were there. It was just a pretty, peaceful, uninhabited-looking little island with white beaches and green jungle.

And there, on the beach of a little cove, was the yellow rubber raft.

The pilot saw it too and said, "That yours?"

"Yeah," Peter said.

"Let's take a look."

"No," Peter said. "Stay away from it."

"I can take you right down over it. They can't hit me."

"No," Peter told him. "Let's get out of here now."

The pilot looked at him, puzzled.

As the plane swung slowly away Peter looked down once more at the raft. Lying peacefully inside it was the dark, rectangular pouch.

"That all you want?" the pilot asked.

"That's all."

"Then let's go back and bug that antiaircraft battery on Huon. We can get shot down twice in one day."

"If you don't mind," Peter said, "I've got a very important appointment."

"Only take a minute," the pilot argued. "Think how happy Tokyo Rose'll be—shooting me down twice in one day."

"Let's disappoint her this time," Peter said. "I don't want to miss my court-martial."

"So they're hanging you, eh?"

"They might," Peter admitted.

That was the longest day he ever spent. And the longest night.

He didn't dare go back to his squadron area for fear of running into Archer, so he hitched a ride from the airfield over to the Six area where a dozen PTs were hiding up a little tributary. He wandered around there until he found a skipper he knew pretty well. The man's name was Mike Myers and had gone through Melville with him.

Peter was afraid to tell anyone, even Mike, the problem, but he arranged to ride Mike's boat on patrol that night and talked Mike into taking him up near Vadang. After the patrol started, Peter decided, he would tell Mike a little more. Not about the pouch, but enough to get Mike to co-operate with him.

The Squadron Six area was a lot better than his. Instead of

muddy trails from the boats to their tents and mess halls and gas dumps, Six had wooden walkways above the mud. Their tents were better too. Peter's outfit had little, leaky tents whose canvas floors had disappeared into the mud long ago. Six's tents were big square jobs with screened sides, proper screened doors on hinges and nice wooden floors high above the mud.

Mike invited him to nap in his tent for the rest of the day, and Peter accepted without any argument at all. He had not slept for thirty hours and needed it.

Peter stopped in the doorway of Mike's tent and looked around at the grandeur of it all. There were no wooden folding cots as his were. No. There were proper beds—two of them —with springs in the mattresses—and bedspreads. There were two chairs, also. And a field desk with a place to write letters under a gooseneck lamp.

It was a mansion! The wood frame walls were six feet high and screened on two sides, solid on the back and front. From there, *good* canvas with no holes in it formed a high roof, stretched on a real wood frame.

That wasn't all. From the ceiling of the tent hung a heavy galvanized bucket with, welded into the bottom of it, a real chrome-plated shower head. This could be lowered by a series of pulleys and ropes so you could fill it and then take a shower. The only thing wrong was that the tent was not high enough for you to stand under the bucket without bumping your head, so Mike had cut a square hole through the floor, lined it with wood, and you could stand down in this hole and take a nice shower.

There was more. On one side of the tent Mike had fixed a jeep windshield, hinged frame and all, as a shelf where he kept his shaving lotion and other toilet articles. And, hinged above the screened sides were twenty-foot slabs of precious plywood, which could be lowered with pulleys to close off the sides and keep the rain out.

High up on the wall, Mike had some sort of experiment

going. On a shelf up there were dozens of glass bottles full of water with fish swimming around. All sorts of little fish, Peter saw. From each bottle a long length of small-diameter plastic tubing—the slimy kind—went down to the floor where Mike had a little air pump. This was running now, making a faint plopping sound, and sending streams of bubbles of air up through the tubes and into the glass bottles. As Peter took off his shoes and went to bed, he wondered how Mike found time enough to fight the war with all the work he had to do fixing up this palatial tent and taking care of all those fish.

Mike woke him about dusk and they went down to the boat. "Pretty swank place you've got here," Peter told him.

"So we leave in about a week. So do you. I guess I'll have to eat all those fish."

"Where're we going?"

"On up the islands. Maybe to the Philippines."

"That's going to be a ride," Peter said.

After they got under way Peter got Mike down into the skipper's cabin and told him what had really happened. At first Mike couldn't believe it. "You mean Archer put the rafts over the side just because the boat was aground?" he asked incredulously.

"And—put the codes and charts in the rubber boat."

"What is he? Crazy? Or scared?"

"I don't know, Mike. I sometimes wonder if he's in the same world with the rest of us."

"The only cure for that guy is to throw the book of regulations over the side and let him figure out a few things for himself. Well, anyway, you're through with him now."

"What do you mean?"

"For losing the codes! He'll get put *under* the jail! Why do they send guys like that out here, Pete? And give 'em command of a boat when they've never heard a shot fired in anger. It beats me."

Peter then told him how he was going to get the codes

back. When he finished, Mike stared at him as though he were crazy.

"You're going to *swim* over to Vadang? You won't make it, Pete. If the sharks don't get you, the Japs will."

"I'll stream some shark repellent as I go along. And I have no intention of strolling around. I'll get that pouch and get out of there."

Mike kept staring at him. "Why are you sticking your neck out, Pete?" he asked. "You didn't lose those codes, Archer did. Why be a hero for a guy like that?"

"It's not important who lost 'em, Mike. Let's just get 'em back before the Japs find 'em."

"So why doesn't Archer go get 'em back?"

"He doesn't even know they're gone."

Mike shook his head slowly. "I wouldn't do what you're trying to do for my best friend, much less a rock-head like Archer. Okay, hero, what do you want *me* to do?"

"Just get me in there without them seeing you. Then circle around, clear of the island, long enough for me to get 'em and get out."

"I can't go in much closer than a thousand, maybe fifteen hundred yards. Can you swim that far?"

"I got a merit badge for swimming."

"Did you get two merit badges? You've got to swim back, you know."

"No, I'll have the rubber boat."

"You're nuts," Mike said. "They'll see you in that boat and drill holes in you."

Peter hadn't thought of that and suddenly the whole adventure began to scare him. But, he asked himself, what else could he do? "I'll get back," he said. "You just keep coming around."

"I still think you're crazy, Pete. But if you make it—and I don't think you will—what you ought to do when you see that Archer again is to step right up and belt him in the teeth."

"Nothing would give me more pleasure," Peter told him, thinking about it.

The quartermaster stuck his head down the hatch and said, "Vadang coming up, Cap'n."

Peter stripped down to his shorts and went up on the foredeck.

The moonlight startled him. He had never seen it so bright, so clear. And the moon hung up there blazing on the water he had to swim through—almost like an enemy searchlight—with the close, bright stars all around the sky. Why, he wondered, couldn't it have rained this night the way it did almost every other night?

Mike called softly from the bridge, "This is as close as we can go, Pete. Any closer and we'll hit something and then all of us'll get it."

"Okay," Peter called back. "See you soon."

Instead of diving, he lowered himself off the bow and down into the dark, warm water. As he started to swim toward the island he felt the wash of Mike's boat as he put her astern and backed slowly away.

He had been swimming for a long time, using a slow-stroke steady crawl, before he paused for a moment to see how he was doing.

Peter was appalled. The island still seemed *miles* away. He turned to look back at the boat.

It had disappeared! Vanished. There was no sign of it and no sound of it.

This was the quietest place Peter had ever been in. The sea was calm so there wasn't even the comforting sound of breaking waves. There were, too, none of the land sounds—the jungle sounds of birds squawking or animals grunting or screaming or barking or jabbering. There wasn't a sound here except that of his own breathing.

He was trapped. He and Mike had figured approximately how long it would take him to swim to the island, get the pouch and swim back, so Mike wouldn't come back in this water for a long time. There was nothing for it but to go on toward Vadang—just go on swimming as long as he could.

He put his head down and started the slow, steady crawl. Once, underwater, he opened his eyes. He didn't do that again. The water was streaked and blotched with lines and patches of phosphorescence. His own arms looked as though they were trailing filmy, thin green gauze as they swept down through the water, and below him in the water, things moved, leaving curving streaks of green or roiling green explosions.

The next time he stopped to look around he found himself almost into the little cove. He could see the dark wall of the jungle beyond the white sand beach and, at the far end, the yellow boat.

He started swimming toward it fast and suddenly stopped. What if they had found it, taken the codes out, but left the boat there as decoy for just such an attempt as this? They would be squatting up there in that dark jungle, a hundred guns covering the beach.

There was only one thing going for Peter. The moon was behind him, shining into their faces—if they were waiting for him. He started swimming again, but now he dog-paddled, keeping his arms and legs below the water and only his head above it.

It was a slow and terrifying journey, but at last his moving knees struck the sand. Now he crawled along the bottom through the shallowing water toward the boat lying so peacefully there on the beach.

When the water ran out from under him he stayed flat on the ground and used his elbows and knees to shove himself on toward the boat. Finally he reached out and grabbed one of the lifelines which were looped along the gunwales.

With the thin rope in his hand he was suddenly paralyzed with fear. Suppose, he thought, this is all they're waiting for. With their whole field of fire converging on this boat, they were just sitting up there in the jungle waiting for it to move.

Peter found some strength somewhere and began to pull on the rope.

The noise of the boat scraping across the sand was *enormous*. A terrible, grinding, grating noise that seemed to him to be loud enough to be heard all over the island.

Then it stopped as the boat slid out over the water.

Peter raised up high enough to see that the pouch was still there and then began to swim frantically away, pulling the boat along by the rope.

He had gone about a hundred yards when another fear hit him and he stopped moving and looked back at the silent island.

The smart thing for the enemy to do, he suddenly realized, was to take the code out of the pouch, copy it, and then put it back. That way, the Navy wouldn't suspect that the code was broken and would go on using it. That was the smart thing to do.

There was one advantage for Peter if they had thought of that. They would *want* him to come and get the pouch. They would *want* him to think that they had not found it. Thus they wouldn't molest him in any way when he came to get it.

He would have to go back to the island. He couldn't just assume that they had found the boat.

Peter raised his face well clear of the water and turned it slowly from side to side, feeling the faint wind on his wet cheeks. It was still from the west, blowing toward Vadang, and steady.

He left the boat floating there and swam back to the beach.

In the moonlight his own tracks, the deep elbow and knee dents and the trail of his body, were clear. So was the faint imprint where the boat had lain. Staying low Peter walked slowly along, around and around where the boat had been until, at last, the debris of the jungle so littered the sand that he could not have seen tracks if there had been any.

He didn't believe that they could have found the boat, walked to it, taken the pouch out, walked back, then walked

again to the boat to leave the pouch and walked back again.
The sand was too smooth and clean and unmarked—and
uniform for yards around.

Peter turned and ran from the rim of the jungle, splashing
out into the warm sea. He grabbed the drifting boat by the
lifeline and swam away from Vadang as hard as he could—
straight out into the moonlit emptiness of the Bismarck Sea.

He swam that way for a long time and then stopped to look
back. Vadang seemed dark and silent and faraway.

He pulled himself up into the boat and was about to reach
for the pouch when he suddenly stopped himself. Perhaps
the intelligence people could tell by the fingerprints whether
or not the pouch had been opened since Murph had closed it.

Peter got out the little paddle, attached the handle to it
and began paddling along, the bow of the rubber boat lifting
high.

He was happily singing as loudly as he could:

"Oh, a capital ship for an ocean trip . . ."

When a voice from behind him joined in:

"Was the 'Walloping Window-blind.'
No gale that blew dismayed her crew
Or troubled the Captain's mind."

The PT boat was almost on top of him, looming up dark
and enormous in the moonlight.

11

Squadron

Six boats sailed very short patrols, Peter decided enviously,
as Mike nosed his boat into her berth before midnight.

By one in the morning the boat had been secured and Peter
and Mike were flemished down in the elegant beds in Mike's
tent.

Just before going to bed Mike had shown him still another bit of swank. Under each of the beds there was a sliding tray. You pulled a short lanyard and this tray came sliding out with all the goodies on it: A flashlight, a fire extinguisher bottle, first-aid kit, a Smith & Wesson .38-caliber revolver (he must have stolen it from the aviators), and a .30-caliber carbine.

Peter looked at this arrangement with admiration, thinking of his own tent, with his carbine hanging from a rope over his bed and getting so rusty he doubted if it would shoot. On the other hand, was all this artillery necessary? It had been months since any Japs had infiltrated the lines and gotten into the tents of any of the PT squadron people.

Mike turned out the light and, for a little while, they lay in bed discussing the boats and the war and the thing at Vadang, but then Mike drifted off to sleep.

It must have been almost two o'clock in the morning, Peter figured later, when he saw the shadow of a moving man fall across the floor of the tent and then heard the sound of footsteps on the wooden steps outside.

Mike must have heard it too, for Peter saw him stir in the other bed and raise himself on his elbows.

After it was all over Peter wondered if, at any time, he could have stopped it or, at least, made it a little less gruesome. He decided that he could have but was glad that he had not.

Without so much as a polite knock on the door, the man flung it open and strode into the tent. Peter saw Mike reaching down for the carbine and at the same time recognized the man. It was Adrian Archer. Peter made a little hissing noise for Mike not to shoot him as Archer, striding as though in a parade or something, came on into the tent.

Then, in a loud and commanding voice, Archer bawled, "Is Ensign Peter Brent in . . ."

The "here" trailed off as Archer strode into the square, deep hole Mike had cut into the floor of the tent. The sharp edge of the hole must have banged him across the shins for they heard him groan with pain as he collapsed into the hole.

Peter and Mike both raised themselves on their elbows and looked at Archer sitting in the hole, the moonlight strong on him. He was rocking back and forth with pain and, Peter thought, humiliation.

Then all his Navy indoctrination returned with a rush. This was no place or position for a commissioned officer in the United States Naval Reserve. It was undignified.

Archer came up out of the hole like a rocket and started to bawl out his question again.

But he came up too fast, too straight.

The sound it made was rather odd, for the heavy steel bucket was full of water for Mike's next bath and as Archer rammed his head against the shower head the sound was a little like *clung*.

It drove Archer back down into the hole and they watched him down in there slowly moving his head back and forth as though to find out if it would move.

Again, as the pain subsided, the indignity of it all swept over Archer. But this time, instead of rushing straight up out of the hole, he came up fast and with dignity to the left.

This time it sounded like a miniature war as Archer's head slammed into the shelf made out of the clear glass of the jeep windshield. There was the solid smack of head against glass, then the rattling of bottles as they danced around and fell over.

The windshield folded up on its hinges and unfolded straight back down and hit him, and this time the broken bottles of foo-foo juice and indigestion medicine poured down on him as he collapsed back into the hole.

The man just wouldn't stop. Wiping the gunk off his face, he came clawing out of there, grabbing anything for a handhold.

He grabbed the rope that held the shower bucket up against the top of the tent. If he had held on to it, Peter decided later, it wouldn't have happened, but when the rope went slack Archer turned it loose.

The heavy steel fire bucket with the chrome shower head welded into its bottom held two and a half gallons of water. It fell like a pile driver straight down on Archer and drove him, like a pile, straight down into the hole. Then it rolled over and poured the water on him.

That did it. Archer must have decided that he was being ambushed, for now he assumed all the cunning and caution of a Marine combat infantryman. He came creeping out of the hole, slowly and silently—except for the water dripping on the floor—and, as a good Marine would, got out of open territory and up against the wall of the tent.

Now he was in deep shadow and they could no longer see him. But he was evidently playing it smart, creeping cautiously along the wall toward the door, and so silently that only the drip-drip of the shower water marked his progress.

But then the glass bottles with the fish swimming around in them began leaping, one by one, off the high shelf. They fell, spilling water and fish, through a band of moonlight and disappeared into the dark shadow where Archer was. Peter and Mike could hear them smashing on the floor. When they had all come down, they could hear a number of odd sounds: the little motor still pumping away, but with the air hissing out of the plastic tubes like the sound of snakes; the fish, not knowing where they were, flapping around wetly on the floor; and Archer, taking deep, agonized breaths.

They could see nothing in the darkness so they sat up in the beds and peered.

Suddenly Archer came rearing up out of the darkness and into the band of moonlight.

He had become absolutely wild as he fought against the slimy, wet, hissing tubes that now entangled him. He tore at them with his hands and all the time kept up a fantastic sort of writhing dance.

In all this grabbing and pulling he must have caught the rope that held up the plywood.

Mike whispered frantically, "Look out!" and Peter just had time enough to lie down flat.

The plywood was three quarters of an inch thick, six feet wide and twenty feet long and was hinged at the top of the tent along the twenty-foot length.

It fell with rapidly gathering momentum, went over Peter with a vicious "whoosh," and slammed Archer and his tubes up against the side of the tent, pinning him there.

When that was all over there was no sound except the hissing of the tubes, the flapping of the sad fish, the drip of water off Archer and a sort of muffled, odd noise as Mike and Peter rammed their faces down into the pillows because they couldn't keep from laughing any longer.

They didn't see Archer get out from under the plywood, free himself of the tubes, and on his hands and knees, a broken man, crawl to the door, slide out of it and disappear.

When he could, Peter took the pillow away and sat up. Outside in the moonlight Archer was standing perfectly still, some of the slimy tubes still dripping from him.

Mike, too, was sitting up, looking at Archer. "Well," he whispered, "that's the end of him."

"No," Peter said. "He's got to come back and try again. He's got to. Or he'll go through life a broken and bitter man."

Archer came back. They watched him strip the slimy tubes from his neck, squeeze some of the water out of his uniform, straighten himself into a military posture and come striding back to the tent.

Peter and Mike collapsed into the beds.

Archer's hard shoes crashed up the two wooden steps of the tent but then stopped.

There was a most polite, quiet little knock on the door. And a polite voice asked, "Is Ensign Peter Brent in there?"

Mike, Peter decided, did it very well. For a long moment

he didn't do anything. Then he rolled over in bed with a sleepy groan.

Archer asked again, "Is Ensign Peter Brent in there?"

Mike raised up slowly and his voice was full of sleep as he said, "Wha . . . at? Who?"

"Peter Brent?"

"Oh. Oh, yeah," Mike said. Then he said, "Peter! Wake up! Somebody wants to talk to you!"

Peter went along with it, rolling over slowly and saying, "Who wants to talk to me? What's the matter?"

"I don't know," Mike said. "Somebody."

"It's me, Archer, Mr. Brent."

"Oh. Hi, Adrian." Peter swung out of the bed and then, because he didn't want Archer ever to know, he added, "Be out in a minute."

Archer must have found out about the missing codes, Peter thought as he pulled on his shoes. Perhaps he had also found out about the missing Murphy and had probably already put the little Irishman in the brig. He might even have drawn up court-martial charges against him.

The fish were still flapping wetly around and the tubes were still hissing as Peter left the tent and joined Archer in the moonlight.

"What are you doing over in this area?" Archer demanded in that cold way of his.

"We've got to get a tug to pull the boat off," Peter said.

"I would prefer it if you would notify me when you want to leave the squadron area. It might have occurred to you, Mr. Brent, that you also left your post of duty while on watch. I consider this a very serious breach of the regulations."

"What do you think the enemy is going to do to a PT boat with a hole in her hull stuck in the mud off the Morobe River?"

"That's not the point. You were on watch, and you left without permission. So did Murphy. This is flagrant disobedience of orders."

"I brought him with me," Peter said. "I've found out, Mr. Archer, that if you want a favor from anyone—like a tug or spare parts—Murph and Mitch, the bosun, always know who to talk to."

"Then you had better prepare yourself to do without the services of Murphy."

Peter looked at this cold man in the moonlight. "Why?"

"Because I'm preferring charges for a general court-martial against him."

Peter felt oddly cold all over. Cold and remote and suddenly stronger than he really was. "Why?" he asked.

"For the careless loss of top-secret codes, which, if found by the enemy, could cause the loss of many ships and men."

"Was it all Murph's fault, Adrian?" Peter asked.

"Of course!"

"Adrian," Peter said quietly, "I don't know what you think a war is, but I'm going to tell you what it is not. You're out here to fight the Japs, not the men in your boat."

For the second time since he had known him Archer seemed to have an emotion. It showed in his low, furious voice. "What do you mean by that?"

"I mean that so far all you've done in this war is read off regulations to the men, parade your authority, and act like a fool."

Archer stood in the moonlight and looked at him for a long, silent moment. When he spoke again there was no more emotion. "I can prefer charges against you for insubordination, leaving your watch station, and—"

Peter interrupted him. "I wouldn't," he said.

"I'm not going to," Archer went on. "But I will accept and will forward, recommending approval, your request for a transfer from my command. In the morning, Mr. Brent."

"I stay with *Slewfoot*," Peter said quietly.

"Then you force me to prefer those charges."

"Did you give Murph orders to put those codes in the rubber boat, Mr. Archer?"

"Of course."

"Did you give him orders to take them out again?"

Archer started to say something and then stopped and thought for a while. "He should have known enough to take them out. Do I have to give an order for every detail?"

"Suppose somebody at Murphy's trial tells how you ordered those codes to be dropped into the boat just because we were aground but, at the time, in no danger of being taken by the enemy? Suppose the judges decide that the codes were your responsibility, not an enlisted man's?"

"You talk as though I were being court-martialed instead of Murphy "

"Perhaps you will be," Peter said.

"Mr. Brent, your insubordination is going to force me to take action against you."

"No, it isn't," Peter told him. "I have the codes."

"How did you get them?"

"That doesn't matter. The thing is I have them. So let's just forget the whole thing." He turned back toward Mike's tent, but then stopped and said, "And unless you want to get shot, you'd better knock before you come into a tent, Mr. Archer."

B O O K   T W O

The Sea

1

Slewfoot
was a sad boat as, at last, she sailed again from the mouth
of the Morobe and into the Pacific on what was to be her
longest patrol.

In the days it had taken to repair her hull and get her out
of that mud, Peter had watched her superb crew break into
pieces like a china plate dropped on a brick floor.

And Adrian Archer was the man who dropped and broke it.

One of the broken pieces was made up of Mitch, the bosun;
Stucky on the 40-millimeter; and, oddly, Sam. These three
were the closest to violence and mutiny against the Captain.

More moderate were Sko, the Preacher and the Professor,
but, to Peter, their moderation seemed more dangerous than
the evident hatred for Archer shown by Mitch's group. As the
boat moved through the dark night, Peter wondered what was
going to happen when Sko and the Preacher and the Professor
got to the end of the line. They were for giving Archer a
chance to show what he could do in a fight before they finally
judged him. What was their judgment going to be if Archer
failed them and failed the boat?

Then there was the broken piece made up of Jason, Willie,
and Skeeter, who would side with Mitch one day and Sko the
next. In Mitch's tent these three would plot dark mutiny.
In Sko's they would agree to give Archer at least one chance.

Oddest of all the pieces was Goldberg. He sided with neither
Mitch nor Sko, although his hatred of Archer was more bare

and evident than that of any other man aboard. Goldberg seemed to have set himself the task of protecting the kid, Britches, from Archer's onslaughts.

Murph was a little splinter all by himself, skittering around trying to find where he fitted with all the groups but in the end staying closer to Peter, who realized that he, himself, was a splinter without a place.

Since the night of Archer and the tent and the talk in the moonlight, Archer had treated Peter with absolutely correct senior-to-junior, chain-of-command procedure. He showed Peter no hostility—and no friendship. The only times he spoke to Peter were to give him correctly phrased, by-the-book orders. He never discussed the methods or the progress of the repairs or the problem of getting her out of the mud. He never discussed anything. He simply told Peter what to do and, usually, how to do it.

On this night, for the first time, Peter was really afraid. He had been scared many times before, but never afraid, never apprehensive. He had never thought before that the crew of *Slewfoot* would not fight the boat to the best of their ability and courage.

But this crew that had fought as one man was now broken into separate little groups of men who might not, when they had to, pool their strength for their own survival.

The days with Archer had been the worst Peter had ever endured. Because the men had not yet been driven to actual insubordination and mutiny against Archer, they took their hatred of him out on each other. Any little thing—a dropped wrench, a lost bolt, a bent nail—would start a fight. Not just an angry outburst but a savage, murderous fight— between friends of long standing.

As Peter stood on the dark bridge beside the Captain the whole miserable thing came down finally to this: the crew of *Slewfoot* were no longer occupied with sailing her. They were occupied only with their hatred for Adrian Archer.

So, as they cleared the strait and entered enemy water, Peter Brent was afraid.

The night was pitch dark, with rain clouds gathering to windward. On the stern Mitch, Stucky and Sam sat on the depth charges, facing forward so they could see Archer. (He had an annoying way of suddenly appearing right behind a man, and you never knew how long he had been there, or what he had overheard.)

"Who'll know?" Mitch demanded. "We get in a fire fight and somebody turns the thirties or the fifties on him. Who'll know?"

Stucky and Sam were not yet ready to go this far. Mitch called them chicken, but they didn't think it was that, it was only that . . .

Sam said, "Well, maybe nobody will know. But *you'll* know, Mitch."

Down in the engine room Sko and Murph were talking it over, Sko chomping slowly on the big cigar. "Anyway you slice it, Murph, it's murder," Sko said.

"All *right*," Murph yelled angrily. "Isn't what he's doing to us murder? So isn't it better to murder one guy rather than have him murder twelve guys?"

"We're still breathing," Sko said. "And if Mitch doesn't lay off all this yakking I'm going to have to straighten him out."

"That'll be the day," Murph said sarcastically.

"It'll be quite a day," Sko said around the cigar.

Forward of the starboard torpedo racks Goldberg and Britches were standing up. Archer could see them in the darkness, and he had given orders for all hands to stand up at their battle stations.

Britches, whispering, was telling Goldberg what he had heard in Mitch's tent. "He said the only way was to get rid of him. You know how I mean?"

"I know how you mean," Goldberg said.

"And Mitch was griping because you wouldn't come in with them," Britches told him. "Mitch said he didn't see how you could take the treatment he's been giving you and not come in with them."

"I'm kind of used to it, Britches," Goldberg said. "They've been picking on me and my folks for several thousand years. You get used to it."

"Do you think Mr. Brent knows what's going on?"

"He knows."

"Who's telling him?" Britches demanded, not liking the idea.

"Nobody's telling him. He just knows."

"Then why doesn't he do something?"

"You can't stop a man from thinking," Goldberg told him. "But if Mitch starts to do anything besides think, Peter'll stop him."

"Do you know . . ." Britches' voice began to squeak so he stopped and started over again. "Do you know what they do to you for mutiny on the high seas?" he asked, his voice under control, but full of awe.

"They take you out and shoot you," Goldberg said.

He turned then and looked down at Britches and decided that things were pretty cockeyed when a kid only seventeen years old could be eight thousand miles from home fighting a war in the dark.

Willie stuck his head out of the radar shack and said, "Bogey, Captain. Range two thousand, bearing two nine three." As Willie started to go back to the scope Archer turned and said, "When reporting objects on the radar give the range, bearing, number of objects, size of objects, course and speed of objects, and your estimate of purpose, Williams."

"Looks like a little *daihatsu* to me, going toward New Guinea."

"On what course, Williams?"

Willie wished that Archer understood a little more about how a radar worked. He had picked this tiny bogey out of the snow and didn't think that many radar operators would have seen it at all and here he was getting a bad time from the Captain because he didn't know what the enemy crew had had for chow. "Gosh, Captain," Willie said plaintively, "the blip's so small and moving so slow I can't figure out all that stuff."

"Then don't report it until you can," Archer said.

"Those little *daihatsus* can't make more than seven or eight knots," Peter said, working the Is-Was board. "Your closing course is two eight six."

"It's not possible to determine a closing course, Mr. Brent, without knowing the speed of the boat."

"We generally go in around fifteen hundred rpm," Peter said. "Above that makes too much noise. At fifteen hundred the course is two eight six."

Without answering, Archer shoved the throttles forward. Peter watched the tach needles move past 1500 and go on to almost 1900, *Slewfoot* throwing herself forward now at 35 knots.

"What is my closing course, Mr. Brent?" Archer asked.

Peter turned the Is-Was. "Two eight nine," he said. He knew exactly what Sko was doing—giving that cigar a beating as his engines labored against the mufflers.

"Give me a bearing and depth for torpedoes," Archer commanded.

Peter stared at him in the dark. "*Torpedoes?* A *daihatsu* is only about fifty feet long."

"So is the conning tower of a submarine," Archer reminded him coldly.

Peter worked out sets for all four torpedoes and Archer passed the word to the Preacher and Goldberg.

Goldberg was disgusted. "So now we're killing mosquitoes with a shotgun," he told Britches as they ground the speed, set the depth into the torpedo mechanisms.

Sko came up out of the engine room, the cigar stern in his teeth. Peter could tell from ten feet away that Sko was mad.

He stopped abaft the bridge, planted his feet apart, slammed the cigar to an upward tilt and said, loud and clear, "Somebody's wrecking my engines running 'em so fast with the mufflers on."

Archer turned slowly around from the wheel and faced him. "Your duty station is in the engine room. And, on patrol, you will wear a life jacket and helmet."

Sko stood there a moment longer, the cigar belligerent, then turned and went below. Peter, knowing what he was going to do, turned to watch the three tachometers. Slowly and evenly the revs dropped back until they were at the maximum rpm with the mufflers on.

Archer saw this too and angrily shoved the throttles forward. The tach needles did not move, the sound of the muffled engines did not change, the speed of the boat remained the same.

"Make a note of that, Mr. Brent. Manual control of the engine speed assumed without authority."

"I'll make a note," Peter said.

Archer turned to the radar shack. "Have you had a recognition signal from the bogey?"

"No, sir, and I don't expect to get one," Willie told him.

Archer turned to the intercom and said, "Man your battle stations. All hands *will* wear life jackets and steel helmets. Life jacket ties *will* be two-blocked. All shirt sleeves *will* be rolled down and buttoned."

In the darkness the men moved around, picking up life jackets and helmets and putting them on. All except Goldberg. He put on the helmet, cocking it as much as you can cock a steel bucket, but he had not even brought his life jacket on deck.

Archer called down, "Goldberg, report to the bridge."

"Why get eaten out for a life jacket?" Britches whispered to Goldberg. "Put it on before he reams you."

Goldberg just grinned at Britches and climbed up to the

bridge. "You send for me?" he asked, his voice as belligerent as Sko's cigar.

"I ordered you to put on your life jacket," Archer told him.

This interested Peter and he stood beside Archer and watched Goldberg. Once before, Goldberg had been told—by Jonesy—to put on his life jacket and Goldberg had said, "Skipper, if it's okay with you I don't want to wear a life jacket." Jonesy had let it drop.

Archer did not. When Goldberg just stood there in silence, Archer said coldly, "Well?"

"I don't wear life jackets," Goldberg said.

Now, Peter thought, this is the time to let this thing drop; leave it alone.

Archer said, "I order you to put on your life jacket."

Goldberg said, as though telling a bedtime story, "One time in The Slot I helped pick up the crew of a boat that had been sunk. They were all alive, for a while. But the sharks had eaten them right up to the life jackets so they didn't live long and they didn't *want* to live at all. Since then I don't wear life jackets."

"As long as you're in the Navy and under my command you *will* wear a life jacket when at your battle station."

"As long as I'm on this boat," Goldberg said quietly and with no anger, "and it's afloat, I don't need a life jacket. When the boat goes down and I'm in the water, I'm not in the Navy any more. I'm just a guy named Goldberg and I don't want those sharks eating half of me and leaving the rest to die. I want 'em to take it all, *right now*."

Goldberg turned and climbed off the bridge and went forward to his torpedo racks. Britches whispered, "What'd he do to you?"

"He's not going to do anything."

"Are you going to put it on?"

Goldberg shook his head, his skull sliding back and forth inside the helmet.

"Put Goldberg on report for direct disobedience of orders," Archer told Peter.

Peter looked at him in the dark and wondered what sort of man he was to be fiddling around with petty details while the boat was closing fast on a target that might start shooting anytime now. "Let's get on with the war," he said quietly, turning and going aft to the radar shack. He studied the scope for a moment and asked, "What's it look like to you, Willie?"

"Just one of those little barges sneaking in the way they do. Why doesn't he go ahead and sink it and get on with the patrol?"

"He is," Peter said.

By the time he got back to the bridge the word had passed from one end of the boat to the other that Goldberg was going to be court-martialed for refusing to put on a life jacket. And, for the first time, all hands now knew why Goldberg had always refused to wear one.

When Sko, in the engine room, heard it he climbed angrily off the tractor seat, grabbed a life jacket and went up through the forward hatch. He marched over to Goldberg and shoved the jacket at him. "Put this on, you big ape. Why get your neck in a noose over a little thing like this?"

"It's headed for a noose anyway, so what difference does it make?" Goldberg asked.

"Put it on, Gerry," Sko said.

Goldberg laughed at him in the dark. "Go spit in that fancy tin hat."

Sko left the jacket on the racks and went below.

Peter said quietly, "Barge. Dead ahead."

Archer looked forward and saw the dark outline of the little *daihatsu* with the unmistakable long, sweeping line from bow to stern. She was putting along at about 7 knots and was now about three hundred yards away.

"Open fire?" Peter asked.

"I don't fire on an unidentified object," Archer said. "That may be one of our own ships, Mr. Brent."

"What are you going to do, run up alongside and ask them who they are?" Peter asked, his irritation showing.

"I am going to close until I identify," Archer said.

"I've seen and sunk a lot of these *daihatsus*. If you don't jump them first they can get pretty rambunctious," Peter told him.

Mitch and Stucky were standing by the Bofors, ready to fire, as the barge got bigger and bigger. They were so close now they could hear the low, slow sound of the barge's engine. They couldn't make out anyone aboard, but they knew that behind those low, sweeping sides the enemy was waiting.

"What's the *matter* with him?" Mitch asked crossly. "Is he going to write up another court-martial before we sink that critter?"

Archer called down to Willie, "Anything on the IFF?"

"Nothing," Willie said.

"Nothing, *sir!*" Archer reminded him.

"Listen, Adrian," Peter said, looking at the barge now less than a hundred yards away, "out here you shoot first and ask questions later. You'd better open . . ."

The barge opened first. Suddenly, from stem to stern, the long side began to flicker with the muzzle blasts of rifles and machine guns. The water ahead of them was suddenly pocked with little white splashes and then they got the range and Peter could hear the bullets hitting the boat, ripping into the plywood and pinging off the racks and the gun mounts.

"Open fire! Open fire!" Archer yelled.

Then, before Peter could stop him the fool yanked *Slewfoot* around, putting her broadside to the barge.

Every gun that could aim at the barge opened up so that *Slewfoot*, too, seemed to be on fire. The brass empties and clips poured out, the cannon shells made an odd, hollow clang as they hit the deck.

Peter heard somebody say in a high, surprised voice, "I'm hit. Goldberg, I'm hit." Then he saw the kid fall over against the torpedo rack.

A deck gun was blazing from the barge now, the muzzle blast a big yellow ball of fire.

Jason was raking the deck, swinging the .50s slowly back and forth and giving it to them in short bursts so the barrels of his guns wouldn't melt.

Stucky was slamming the 40-millimeter shells into her right at the waterline, each one tearing a piece out of the wooden barge.

Sko was waiting for the signal to take the mufflers off and *move*. It didn't come.

Willie heard a bullet hit close beside him. Splinters of plywood rained down on him and the radar and then bits of metal. He heard something arcing and fusing and was looking up when the lights went out.

The barge was going down. Straight down, neither bow- nor stern-heavy—just sinking straight down, ripped apart all along the waterline by the Bofors and 20.

The rifle and machine-gun fire dribbled to a stop, but the deck gun got off one more round before she sank.

This last shell came straight over the water at point-blank range and struck *Slewfoot* astern, entering her about two feet above the waterline and ten feet forward of the transom.

Fortunately for Skeeter and the Professor they were both at the forward end of the engine room when the shell came in. Sko, of course, was in his tractor seat above the center engine.

The thin plywood hull of *Slewfoot* did not offer the exploding mechanism in the nose of the shell enough resistance to trigger it, but when it struck the steel casing of the reduction-gear boxes it exploded. The concussion knocked out the lights, slammed Skeeter and the Professor to the deck and swept Sko out of his seat and down between the No.1 and No.2 engines.

It did more than that. It shattered both the V-drives of the outboard engines and destroyed the reduction-gear boxes.

At the time, the engines were turning over at 1500 rpm, but when the load was suddenly removed, with no way for all that power to be transferred into the shafts and propellers, the engines ran wild. All three of them began revving up, the sound they made changing into a scream.

Sko, Skeeter and the Professor, still dazed and hurt, fought their way up in the darkness to the controls and, one by one, shut down the engines.

Sko knew it was too late, for as the engines slowed and stopped, he could hear the grinding of the ruined main bearings.

Then it was silent down there.

Slewfoot lay dead in the water, wallowing and hurt, as the rain closed in on her.

2

For a long moment the only sound on *Slewfoot* was the beating of the rain; no one moved or talked, they just stood where they were, every one of them waiting, staring aft at the place where the gasoline tanks were. Waiting for the blinding, jarring, destroying flash. But as *Slewfoot* wallowed in the moving sea and the rain fell from the black sky and there was no flash the men began slowly to move.

Peter ran down from the bridge to the starboard rack where Goldberg was on his knees beside Britches, trying to shield the boy from the falling rain.

In the pitch-darkness it looked to Peter as though Britches had been torn apart and was now just a mass of blood.

"Is he dead?" Goldberg asked in a faint, remote voice. "Peter, is he dead?"

Peter felt down into the warm blood and found Britches' throat with his fingertips. "No. He's alive." Peter stood up and called over to the Preacher. "Preacher, help Gerry get the boy below." Then he said to Goldberg, "I've got to see to the boat. I'll bring the first-aid kit."

Goldberg slid his arms under the boy and lifted him, saying, "I don't need any help."

As Peter went down the forward hatch on the double he heard Archer yelling, "Don't leave your battle stations without orders."

This sudden loud voice seemed to daze and paralyze the men who had begun to drift away from the guns. They stopped moving and looked up at Archer who was still standing on the bridge, the wheel in his hands as though *Slewfoot* were still alive.

Except Goldberg. Britches seemed weightless in the big man's arms as he strode through the rain toward the amidships hatch.

Archer came down from the bridge and stood, blocking Goldberg's passage.

What Archer intended to say or intended to do no one would ever know. The men stood in silence, watching, as Goldberg came on through the rain and found Archer standing there, blocking the way.

Goldberg did not strike the officer. All he did, as the men would swear, was shift his grip on Britches so he could carry him with one arm and then, with his freed arm, he put his big hand on Archer's chest and pushed.

Archer moved straight aft, his two feet sliding along on the wet deck, for about four feet before he went over backwards.

As Goldberg went down the hatch with Britches, Mitch and Stucky came forward to where Archer was lying, flat on his back. They got him under the armpits and jerked him straight up and set him down on his feet.

"Did you see that?" Archer demanded. "Did you see Goldberg . . ."

Mitch stepped around in front of him and interrupted him in a quiet, firm voice. "You tripped on that stanchion," Mitch said, "and fell."

Stucky said, "Just tripped and fell."

"No! Goldberg . . ."

"You tripped, Mr. Archer," Mitch said.

Archer looked at the two men for a moment and then, silently, he pushed past them and went to the bridge. There he seemed to become himself again. "Secure from battle stations. Divisions report casualties and damage."

Willie got the emergency lights on as Peter entered the engine room. Skeeter's face was covered with blood but it was all coming from a small slit in his forehead made either by a fragment of the shell or a flying gear tooth.

Sko was aft, shaking his head at the sight.

"Can we get under way?" Peter asked, looking at the mess of torn and broken metal, rubber belts, shorn gear teeth lying in a bath of oil.

Sko rolled the cigar from one side of his mouth to the other. "If we had a paddle."

"What happened?" the Professor asked. "Sounded to me like they got in the first shot."

"They did," Peter said and turned back to Sko. "How about the engines?"

"They were going like banshees," Sko told him. "If they've got any bearings left it'll be a miracle."

"Anything you can rig up to get us moving?"

"Not before daylight," Sko told him. "If ever."

"Do the best you can. We won't look good out here in the daylight." He turned toward the door, saying, "Britches got hit."

"Oh, no!" the Professor said. "Bad?"

"I don't know," Peter said, leaving.

Peter stopped by the captain's cabin for the first-aid kit.

A bullet coming through the hull had struck the silver-framed picture of Jonesy's parents, he noticed, as he got the kit and hurried into the dayroom.

It was an awful wound. The heavy-caliber bullet must have ricocheted off the torpedo rack for it had torn upward through Britches' left arm and shoulder and then up the side of his neck, leaving a bloody furrow to beyond his ear.

In the dim emergency light Goldberg's face looked like ashes and he was standing beside the bunk rocking back and forth and making a moaning sound in his throat.

Peter glanced at him and felt, as Goldberg did, helpless. In a flash thought he remembered Jonesy, and so many other PT-boat skippers, angrily saying that at the school in Rhode Island they should have been taught a lot less naval etiquette and a lot more about how to save a man's life when he'd been hit.

"He's going to die," Goldberg said in the same remote small voice. "The kid's going to die if we don't do something."

Then Archer's voice was loud and harsh behind them. "Stop blubbering, Goldberg. Are you just going to stand there and let him bleed to death, Mr. Brent?"

He pushed between them and leaned over to look at the wound. "Get out of the light!" he snapped as he picked up the torn arm.

It took Goldberg a moment to react, then he moved toward Archer. "If you hurt him . . ."

Archer looked over his shoulder and said, "I'm going to hurt him, so shut up." Then he turned to Peter, who was holding the first-aid kit. "Well, *open* it!" he said.

Peter got the tin top open and Archer, looking as though he knew what he was doing, got out the rubber tourniquet and deftly wrapped it around Britches' arm, tightening it with the little handles. "Hold this," he told Goldberg. "Just tight enough to stop that blood."

Goldberg took the handles in his big hands and held them, staring down at the arm until the blood stopped pumping out.

"Sam!" Archer yelled. "Boil some water."

"Yes, sir," Sam said and they could hear him rattling pots in the galley. Suddenly there was no more rattling. "There isn't any water," Sam said. "The tanks got hit and it's gone."

Archer turned for a moment to look at Sam and he seemed to have forgotten Britches. "Tell Mitch to spread a tarpaulin and catch this rain in anything that'll hold it," Archer told Sam.

Peter said, "I read somewhere that you don't need to wash out a wound if it's clean. So why waste time for water?"

"I'm not wasting time, Mr. Brent. Britches will need that water to drink."

He turned back to Britches, sprinkling the sulfa powder from the little can into the long wound. "We'd better be ready to give him a shot," he said to Peter. "You stand by with it."

"A shot?" Peter asked.

"Morphine! If it isn't in there I'm going to court-martial this crew."

The little Syrettes were there. Peter got one out and broke the glass nipple off.

"I'll be back in a minute," Archer said. "If he comes to, give him the morphine."

"Where're you going?" Goldberg demanded. "You can't leave him like this."

"To wash my hands," Archer said, taking the little cake of surgical soap out of the kit and going up through the hatch.

Peter and Goldberg looked at each other. "Do you think he knows what he's doing?" Goldberg asked.

"I don't know. But it's more than I know."

"I guess he'll die if we don't do something," Goldberg said.

"I guess so," Peter agreed.

Archer, dripping with rainwater, came awkwardly down through the hatch holding his hands up and away from him and not touching anything. "Get that needle out of there. The big one," he said, pointing with his elbow at the brown canvas surgical kit.

Peter unfolded the kit, which contained a flat metal box of various sized scalpels, some scissors and hemostats, tweezers, probe and a packet of surgical needles. Peter's hands were trembling a little as he tore open the sterile wrapping. Somehow the needles fell out, landing on the bloody bunk.

Archer looked at him coldly and said, with heavy sarcasm, "Nice going, Doctor Kildare. Who's got a lighter?"

Goldberg fished one out of his wet dungarees.

"All right, Mr. Brent," Archer said like a schoolteacher. "Hold that needle with the tweezers and heat it with the lighter. When it's cool, give it to me."

Goldberg held the lighter while Peter picked one of the needles out of the blood and held it in the flame with the tweezers. He started to blow on it to cool it but Archer said, "Don't blow your dirty breath on it! Wave it around."

When it was cool enough Peter gave it to him. "All right," Archer said, "now unwrap the thread and *try* not to drop it or let it touch anything. Including your hands."

This time Peter wasn't shaking. Archer took the thread and very deftly threaded it through the eye of the long, curved needle. Then, holding the thread clear of everything he bent over Britches. "Now," he said, "you two hold the flesh together so I can sew it up. Just press the edges together as I go along. Be careful not to touch the edges where it's raw."

Peter looked down at the long, jagged-edged wound with blood still seeping all through it. He could see the muscles, a pale, awful gray, and at one place the bone, a startling white. Then he looked up at Archer. "Do you know what you're doing, Adrian?"

"Do you know a better way?" Archer asked.

"No."

"Then let's do it my way," Archer said.

Peter and Goldberg leaned together.

The blood was slick and warm under their fingers, but they managed somehow to push the torn edges of the flesh together.

It was the most terrible thing Peter had ever seen. Archer seemed to have no feeling as he jammed the needle through the edges of Britches' flesh, the sharp, blackened point stabbing in past the hairs on the arm and coming out into the bloody area, then jabbing into the other side and coming out through the hairs. But then, with a marvelously deft and quick movement of his fingers, Archer spun a knot into the thread with one hand, the other holding the thread clear, and drew it tight. Then the stabbing needle again.

He had made half a dozen stitches when he suddenly stopped. "Give him a shot," he told Peter. "He's coming to."

Without thinking, Peter wiped his bloody hands on his trousers and got the morphine Syrette. He put the sharp point against Britches' other arm and watched it indent the flesh. And then Peter could not push it on in. He looked up helplessly to find Archer staring at him coldly.

Peter pushed it in and watched the colorless fluid leaving the Syrette. "All of it?" he asked.

"All of it. We've got a long way to go," Archer said.

The brutal stabbing and then the jerking and tightening of the thread went on up Britches' arm. Jason and the Preacher came in and watched; then Sko and Skeeter, the Professor, Mitch, Stucky—all of them. Archer seemed not to know that they were there as he went on stabbing and making the quick, sure knots. "All right," he said finally. "We can hold the rest together with tape."

With swabs and bandage and adhesive, Archer closed the rest of the wound and then gave Britches a shot of penicillin as Goldberg moved him from the bloody bunk to a clean one.

For a moment Goldberg stood looking down at Britches, and then he turned to Archer. "You did a good job," he said.

Archer finished putting away the kit before he turned to

Goldberg and said, "Now there're some matters I want to take up with you, Goldberg. You struck me."

Mitch came out of the shadows in one long stride. He pushed Goldberg aside with a sweep of his arm and stood in front of Archer. "I told you, Mr. Archer, you tripped. We all saw you trip."

"What's this all about?" Peter asked.

"He tripped," Mitch said. "On the stanchion."

"And fell," Stucky said. "We saw him."

Archer ignored them and said, "I'll take this up with you later, Goldberg."

"You do that," Goldberg said, turning back to Britches.

Peter broke the strained silence. "Any chance of moving, Sko?"

"None," Sko said.

"Why not?" Archer demanded.

Sko looked at him, the cigar pointing at him like an accusing finger. "The only place this boat is going is . . . down."

3

As the
storm swept into the Bismarck Sea the wind began to blow from the south-south-east, slanting rain across the wallowing deck and driving *Slewfoot* northward. Archer insisted on a watch being kept on deck, and Murphy was appointed for the hours from midnight until two in the morning. He stood on the bridge now, huddled against the ice-cold rain, and silently cursed the Captain. In the pitch-dark and driving rain he couldn't have seen Grant's Tomb ten feet away. And the entire Japanese Navy couldn't have seen *Slewfoot*, as her gray hull blended with the driving gray sea, her low silhouette blanketed by the waves sweeping past her.

In the engine room it was hard to stay on your feet, for

the deck plates were slimy with oil from the reduction-gear box and the motion of the boat was completely different from that when she was under way. This was a violent, cork-screw motion, awkward and jerky with no indication from which direction the next movement would come.

Peter—stripped down to his rolled-up trousers—Sko, the Professor and Skeeter were working on the wreckage. They cleared away the broken pieces of the gear box and steering mechanism, gathered up the teeth and parts and finally got the oil cleaned up enough to see how severely the whole drive mechanism from the engine shafts to the logs had been damaged.

Peter looked at it in dismay. The belts of both V-drives had been torn to pieces, the reduction-gear box had first been broken open by the shell burst and then the gears and shafts had been totally wrecked by the engines running wild.

"Nothing a week in dry dock won't fix," the Professor said.

Sko pointed the cigar at him. "So where's the dry dock?"

With a wrench and hammer Peter disconnected the tangled remote steering mechanism and connected the balanced rudders to the manual system. As he finished, he said cheerfully, "At least we can steer her." But when he tried to swing the rudders, nothing moved. Sko and then the Professor and Skeeter came to help him, but the four of them could not force either rudder to move an inch. "It must be jammed on the outside," Peter decided.

"Then the shafts are, too," Sko guessed. "We're in trouble, Peter."

They looked at each other. Peter felt as though he had a black curtain across his mind. He could think about right now; even think about the next hour or, by trying, the next day. But the curtain was drawn down black and stern against any thinking beyond that.

At two in the morning Jason, the gunner, went on deck to relieve Murph. The storm was steady now, the rain pouring down, the wind strong and gusty from the south. Jason climbed up to the rolling and pitching bridge where Murph was making no attempt to look around as he squatted in the lee of the structure. Jason joined him and Murph said, "Why don't we get moving? Are we going to sit out here all night?"

"We're going to sit out here longer than that," Jason told him. "The engines are wrecked and so is the steering."

"What's going to happen at daylight?" Murph asked, alarmed.

"Some Jap plane'll sink us," Jason said. "Okay, I relieve you."

Murph got stiffly to his feet. "Watch out for the porpoises," he said and made his way across the wild deck to the hatch.

Murph, starving, went into the galley and found Archer giving Sam a bad time. Sam had brought along only enough supplies to make a snack for the night's patrol. There was bread, some cans of Spam, some grease they called butter, a few tins of sardines, two dozen tasteless chocolate bars, four pounds of ground coffee, six cans of peaches, a packet of two dozen dried eggs, and six little tins of condensed milk.

Sam was trying to explain that he had taken the main food supplies ashore while the boat was on the mudbank to keep them from being ruined, but Archer would not accept that as an excuse. Sam should have put them back aboard, Archer declared.

While those two were busy with their argument, Murph filched one of the chocolate bars—for he felt sure Archer was not going to let Sam make any sandwiches this night—and wandered on into the dayroom where the rest of the deck gang were patching up the bullet holes.

At three-thirty in the morning Peter left the engine room to Sko and climbed up to the radar shack.

Willie had the radio transmitter out of the rack, opened up and spread out on the chart board. He looked tired and defeated as he turned to watch Peter come in.

"How's it going?" Peter asked.

"You push a bullet through one of these things and somehow it doesn't work so good any more." He showed Peter where the bullet had gone through the vitals of the transmitter.

"Can you fix it?"

"I only had six weeks of radio school," Willie reminded him, "and this is a mess."

"How about the spare-parts kit?"

"All I've got are some tubes and condensers and resistors; but, you see, all these sockets are ruined and the whole tuning end is messed up."

"How about the radar?"

"That's okay."

"Well, that's something. Do what you can, Willie. It'd be nice to be able to talk to somebody."

"You're not just beating your gums," Willie said glumly as he turned back to the tangled wreck.

Peter went on up to the bridge, the cold rain feeling good on his bare skin for a moment—then it got too cold. Jason was ducking the flying spray and peering uselessly out into the wet darkness when Peter stepped up beside him.

Slewfoot was not built for this kind of going. With her long, high-bowed speedboat hull, squared-off stern and flat bottom, she rode miserably when she was powerless in a seaway. The waves—which she could have taken in stride with the engines going—were breaking over her, the running water slamming against the racks and turrets and bridge adding spray to the driving rain.

Nor would she stay quartered to the wind as a sailboat, or a sea gull, would have. Instead, the wind blew her this way and that, driving her sometimes head on into the sea, sometimes stern first, oftener just leaving her wallowing, the seas pouring over her.

"Why don't you stand the rest of the watch in the chart house?" Peter yelled through the sounds of rain and sea. Then he added, knowing that Jason was asking a silent question, "I'll tell the Captain."

"Thanks," Jason said, his teeth chattering as he worked his way aft to the comfort of the chart house.

Hanging on to anything he could grab, Peter made his way forward, trying in the darkness to see if the seas were damaging the boat. He couldn't be sure, but as he reached the hatch he thought that *Slewfoot* was taking it pretty well.

He came down through the hatch between waves, letting in only a shower of rainwater.

In the dayroom all the lights were out except the blue battle lamp which always burned at night. In the dim light he could see Goldberg sitting on a couple of life jackets on the deck beside Britches. Peter went over to him and looked at the boy who seemed to be sleeping. Britches' face was dead white and pain was running over it in little ripples every time the boat jarred him. The white bandage was soaked through with blood.

"How's he doing?" Peter whispered.

"Pretty good, I think," Goldberg whispered back. "He was moaning and groaning awhile back, but now he's stopped."

"How about the bleeding?"

"It stopped a couple of hours ago. I guess Archer did a good job."

"Hope so. Look, Gerry, you'd better turn in. It's going to be a long day."

"Yeah," Goldberg said wearily as he pulled himself up and climbed into the bunk above Britches. "If he starts moaning again maybe we ought to give him another shot of that morphine."

"We'd better ask Archer," Peter said.

"Yeah," Goldberg said. "Archer."

In the galley, Sam was cleaning out the empty food cabinets. "What's for chow?" Peter asked.

"Nothing's for chow. I'm in trouble, Peter. I didn't bring the supplies the book says we should have. Archer ate me out."

"We're not going to be out here forever," Peter consoled

him. "Have you got enough for a meal or two for all hands?"

"Archer says nobody gets *anything*. And somebody's already swung with one of the chocolate bars. Murph, I think."

Peter looked at the empty compartments. "Haven't you got anything to eat?" he asked, surprised.

"He's got it. All of it. In his cabin."

Outraged, Peter turned and knocked on the captain's door.

"Come in," Archer said.

Peter went in and saw all the cans of food, the bread and everything else stacked up on the bunk. Archer was sitting at Jonesy's desk making a list of it.

"What's the big idea?" Peter demanded.

"Somebody had already stolen some of this food," Archer told him. "From now on it's going to be under lock and key and every man will get an equal share. Furthermore, I want you to put a lock on the scuttlebutt so that no one can drink water without my permission."

Peter stood looking down at him in amazement. Archer now looked gray and beaten and weak, but his eyes were still glittery and his chin stubborn. "Sometimes I think you're crazy, Adrian."

"I'm not," Archer said without anger.

"Maybe not . . . well, it's no soap on the engines. Both V-drives are wiped out and there's no way to get through the reduction gear. Paddlin' Madeleine home."

"I'm aware of that, Mr. Brent."

"The rudders are jammed, too."

"I know."

"And a bullet took out the transmitter."

"Don't you think I know what's going on aboard this boat?"

Peter was counting to ten as he started to sit down on the bunk.

"You're soaking wet," Archer reminded him.

Peter straightened up and then leaned against the bulkhead. " . . . nine . . . ten," Peter said, aloud. "Now . . ."
He looked down at Archer and wondered what he and *Slew-*

foot and the crew had done to get such a man as commanding officer.

"Adrian," he said, "we're in a lot of trouble and it's the kind of trouble your "black-shoe Navy" doesn't help. The kind of trouble where all of us have got to get along with each other or we get along without each other and come up dead. So how about knocking off all this *I'm*-THE-BOSS nonsense and try being a human being."

Archer turned in the chair and looked up at him as though he were a wayward child. "I don't think you realize yet, Mr. Brent, how much trouble we really are in. Or realize that it is the kind of trouble that demands the sternest and most impartial and impersonal discipline. When you do, we will discuss it further."

"Let's discuss it now," Peter said. "First, why have you posted a watch on deck in weather like this?"

"If you will read the regulations . . ."

Peter interrupted him, trying not to let his anger show, "The regulations are what put us where we are now. So why don't you forget the regulations and just start trying to save this boat and the people in her?"

"You think this is my fault, don't you?" Archer asked.

Peter looked at him for a long moment and wished that he was not so tired and dismayed. It was hard to think about Archer now, but it was necessary. "Yes, I do," he said slowly.

"Suppose that barge had been one of our ships? And we had opened fire on it and sunk it. Whose fault would *that* have been, Mr. Brent?"

"His fault," Peter said. "At night this is PT-boat water. Our ships are not supposed to be in this area at night." He stopped and looked at Archer. "Not your fault, really," he went on, "but there're some things they didn't teach you in Rhode Island and the best way to learn them is by listening— the way the rest of us did."

"Thank you, Mr. Brent. You may go now."

"One more thing. How about giving Britches some more morphine?"

"No more. Unless there's serious infection and pain. Do you want to make a dope addict out of him?"

"You're probably right," Peter said, feeling defeat rolling over him like a slow wave as he turned toward the door. Then he stopped and looked at Archer again. "Adrian, for your own good, take this little piece of advice. Don't go near the rail on dark nights."

Archer stiffened in his chair and, for an instant, his face was drawn with some sort of pain or anger . . . something. "Is that a threat, Mr. Brent?" he demanded.

"That's advice, Adrian," Peter said, and went out.

When Peter went out, Archer got up slowly from the chair and walked over to the door. Taking a key out of his pocket, he locked it, testing the knob. Then he went back to the chair.

On deck, aft, Mitch and Stucky were floundering around, yelling curses at each other and anything else they could think of. Archer had ordered them to rig one of the canvas gun covers to catch the rainwater. The way he had explained it sounded simple enough: catch rain in the fire buckets, dump the fire buckets into the water tank (the bullet holes in it had been plugged). Simple.

It was not simple at all. In the first place, although it was pouring cold rain, not much of it seemed to be falling into the funnel they had made out of the gun cover. The next problem was to keep the fire buckets from being knocked all over the deck by the sweeping waves. And these same waves were knocking them around too. They had managed, in an hour, to pour into the tank about a bucket and a half and, as the storm got worse, they were catching and keeping less and less.

"Belay it," Mitch yelled. "If that idiot wants a drink of water let him come get it himself."

Shivering with cold and bone tired, Stucky and Mitch went below.

They did not see a wave sweep over the quarter and carry away the fire buckets. For a moment they rattled around the depth charge racks, then rolled on around the smoke generator and fell into the sea.

In the little chart house Peter dried his hands and unrolled the chart of the Bismarck Archipelago, pinning it to the table. He plotted in the last known position of *Slewfoot* from Willie's contact report and then broke out the tide tables and checked the winds and currents of the area. These alone would move *Slewfoot* now and they would move her as they willed and not as he or Archer or any man willed.

Slewfoot was in an eddy of the South Equatorial Current which swept in a great band of warm water westward toward the Philippines and the Celebes Sea and then swung north and around to move eastward again above the Equator. This unseen and unfelt movement of the sea was, Peter knew, taking *Slewfoot* a little to the north of west.

Added to the current of the sea *Slewfoot* would also be at the mercy of the southeast trade winds pouring up from the belt of the Roaring Forties and the South Polar ice cap. The winds, like the current, would move *Slewfoot* westward and slightly north.

The combined strength of the two—the current and the wind—over a long period of time would, Peter calculated, move *Slewfoot* at the rate of about 4 or 5 knots.

He paused for a moment, thinking of what Archer had said—that he didn't realize how serious their problem was. He wondered if Archer did. There were only two answers to it. If, tomorrow, *Slewfoot* was sighted by one of our patrol planes she could be saved. Or—and Peter did not see how it could be done—Sko could get her moving under her own power again and she could save herself. But only if Sko did it soon. *Slewfoot* was being driven, by wind and sea, a hundred or more miles a day. If it took Sko too long, there would simply not be enough gas to get her home again.

Peter laid the parallel rulers down on the compass rose at the side of the chart and picked off the course he estimated *Slewfoot* was moving on. Then he walked the rulers across the chart to her last known position.

The sharp, straight edge of the rulers cut through the penciled dot of *Slewfoot's* last position and then went across the Bismarck Sea and on into the Pacific Ocean—on and on until, at last, the rulers came to the Philippine Islands. Peter took a pair of dividers out of the rack, opened them to the degree scale on the chart and began to spin them along the line of the ruler. As the miles mounted up he spun the sharp dividers slower and slower.

Two thousand miles. Two thousand miles of open and hostile ocean. Two thousand miles of the awful wastes of the Pacific now completely dominated by the enemy.

4

At four o'clock in the morning, Peter looked into the dayroom. Sko, Skeeter and the Professor, so tired they had not even stripped off their oil- and water-soaked pants, were sprawled in their bunks. Jason, just relieved of the watch by the Preacher, was taking off his dripping clothes. Goldberg was awake in his upper bunk and Britches was still asleep. Murph's sleep seemed undisturbed by his guilt. Stucky was having a nightmare and Mitch was snoring. Sam was sleeping as usual with one foot out of the bunk and planted firmly on the deck. Only Willie was missing.

Peter found Willie sound asleep, his head down among the parts of the ruined transmitter.

As Peter came back down into the boat, weariness overwhelmed him too. As he went aft he saw that there was still a slit of light from under Archer's door, but there was no sound.

As Peter stripped off his long-wet clothes he prayed for sunshine. If it kept on raining like this, no one would see them on the gray sea.

In his dream, *Slewfoot* drifted through the rain forever and ever.

Angry voices outside his door woke him up.

Mitch, Stucky and Jason were crowded into the narrow passageway in front of Archer's cabin. Archer was standing with his back to the closed cabin door.

"What do you mean, no chow . . . sir?" Mitch demanded.

"Exactly that," Archer said.

"Look, Mr. Archer," Jason said, his voice less angry than Mitch's, "we haven't eaten since yesterday."

Peter squeezed out of his cabin and moved over beside Archer.

"There's very little food aboard," Archer said. "What there is may have to last us a long time. It will be given to you in small amounts at twelve hundred each day. Until it's gone."

Mitch began to laugh. "Man, you talk like we're going to be out here forever."

"We'll be back in Morobe tonight," Stucky added.

"You will be given something to eat at twelve hundred," Archer said and went back into his cabin. They could hear the key turning in the lock.

Mitch was furious. "How about it, Peter? Is he going to get away with that?"

"He's eating it all himself," Stucky decided.

"Calm down," Peter said, "and get out of here. I'll talk to him."

When they had cleared the passageway, grumbling to themselves, Peter knocked on the door. "Brent," he called.

The key turned, and he went in. Archer had not shaved, which made him look even more gray and sick. As Peter started to say something, Archer said, "Before you start sounding off, answer me this. If we are not sighted today what do you think is going to happen?"

Peter laughed. "We'll take a long, lonesome ride."

"Exactly. And if we're going to survive we must save what food we have. We must make it last for days, perhaps weeks, perhaps—months. There isn't much."

"Then why don't you explain that to the men instead of acting like a little Hitler?"

"I leave the popularity contests to you, Mr. Brent."

"Thanks a lot," Peter said and left.

He was startled by the brilliance of the sunshine when he reached the deck. It was a beautiful day, rain-washed and clear and warm, with the gentle southeast trade wind blowing steadily. High, brilliant white clouds drifted unconcerned toward the horizon, and the sea was almost pure blue and the sparkling of the little waves like diamonds.

There was nothing in sight except the sea and the sky. The green lump of New Guinea had disappeared, the long white line of New Britain had gone.

Peter went up to the foredeck and called down the hatch for all hands on deck. The men who were not already topside came trooping up, all unshaved and tired and angry.

As they gathered around him, Peter looked at them one by one. The faces he had known for so long all seemed changed —older, oddly bitter, the tired eyes a little wild, the mouths set and angry.

"Now look, you guys," Peter said, "get with it. We're in a mess and you people are acting like a bunch of spoiled brats."

Peter heard Stucky say in a low voice, "Maybe he's eating chow with the Captain."

Peter pushed through them to the gunner. "You've been riding this boat as long as I have, Stucky. And done some good shooting. All I want from you is more of the same."

He turned back to the others. "Now. Sko, what's chances of getting the engines going?"

"Forget 'em," Sko said.

"Okay," Peter went on, "then here's what I think will happen. With a day like this our patrol planes will spot us from a hundred miles away. It's made in the shade. But we can't take a chance in case they miss us. So the Captain's right. Until we know we've been sighted and help's on the way, we've got to go easy on the chow. Because if we don't get spotted we've got a two-thousand-mile ride, and what little food we've got will have to last the whole way."

Stucky said angrily, "Willie, why don't you fix that transmitter? How'd you get a rate as a radioman if you can't even fix a transmitter."

Willie, instantly furious, turned on Stucky. "You're so smart, you dumb trigger-puller. You fix it!"

"Knock it off," Peter said. Then he looked at them, one by one. "You guys get with this boat, the way you used to be. She's gotten you out of a lot of trouble. Now you get her out of this trouble."

He looked at them again and, slowly, their faces became the faces he had known before—the faces of men he could trust to do what had to be done.

All except Stucky. For some reason, this one would not change, but stood, his face angry and sour, and stared at Peter.

And as Peter walked away from them he heard Stucky yelling at Sam, "It's all your fault, Sam! This boat should be loaded with chow."

As Peter turned and started back, Archer's commanding voice from the bridge stopped both him and the argument.

"All hands! Man your battle stations!"

The words froze them for an instant and then they broke and ran for the guns.

Peter ran up on the bridge beside Archer. "What's up?"

"Listen," Archer said.

Then Peter could hear it. The far, faraway drone of a plane. He got the binoculars out of the chart house and began scanning the sky, starting in the southeast.

The plane was just a dot in the blue sky. It didn't even seem to be moving. "I can't make it out," he told Archer, "but it's coming from the southeast so it must be one of ours."

Peter leaned over the windshield and called, "Spread the flag out across the deck. I think this is one of ours."

As Goldberg and the Preacher broke out the flag and spread it across the foredeck, Goldberg said, "I hope that's a Navy plane. Those Army guys don't know a PT boat from a petunia bed."

"I don't care who he works for. I just want him to see us," the Preacher said.

"Twin-engine bomber," Peter said, studying the plane. "Don't see any rising sun, but it might be there."

"What's his course and altitude?" Archer asked.

"About two eighty and he's *way* up there—ten or fifteen thousand."

Every man aboard except Britches was watching the plane as they stood at the guns, their heads bent back. It looked so unreal up there in the sky. So tiny as it moved along.

"He'll never see us," Stucky told Mitch. "He's too high."

Peter lowered the glasses and was surprised to find Archer sitting in the underway seat abaft the bridge with his eyes closed. Now he opened them and looked up at the plane for a moment. Then Mitch came running up on the bridge. "Why don't we make smoke?" he asked. "Maybe he'd see the smoke."

"With the wind the way it is the smoke would just blow all over us, Mitch. Then he'd never see us," Peter told him.

"I guess you're right," Mitch said and started aft again.

Archer stopped him. "Stand by to make smoke, Mitchell."

Mitch looked from Archer to Peter. "The smoke'll just cover the boat, Adrian," Peter said as quietly as he could.

"I didn't say make smoke. I said stand by to make smoke," Archer said coldly and closed his eyes again.

The plane came steadily toward them, the faraway droning changing slowly to a soft hammering sound. There were no red meatballs on it and at last Peter could recognize it as an Army patrol bomber.

As it came closer the men left the guns and began to jump around on deck, waving their arms and uselessly shouting.

But the high hammering plane went over them swiftly with no change of altitude and continued toward the northwest.

The noise and movement of the men died and slowed and left them standing there, slowly turning their heads as the plane went away with no sign of having seen them.

And then lazily the plane turned and as it turned it nosed down, peeling down out of the sky and coming back toward them.

"I take back everything I ever said about the Army," Mitch told Stucky. "Wonderful outfit! I'm going to give 'em all a medal."

The plane continued to dive as it straightened out of the turn and was now coming directly at them. Peter estimated from the angle of the dive that the plane would pass over them at about a hundred feet. "Hold the flag up so he can see it!" he yelled down to Goldberg.

The men were yelling again and jumping around in pure joy as the plane came on toward them.

Peter was the first to see the little winking lights along the leading edges of the wings. "Get down! Get down!" he yelled as, across the bright blue water, the little vicious white footsteps raced toward *Slewfoot*.

It took the men a few seconds to realize what was happening and, even after they did, they stood a moment longer staring in utter disbelief at the machine-gun bullets striking the water and now seeing the faint lines of the tracers through the sunlight. And then they dived for cover.

Except Goldberg. He stood out on the foredeck, a big, unmissable target and waved the flag, holding out as much of it as he could with his long arms.

The streams of bullets missed *Slewfoot*, slamming past on each side of her.

And then the little spinning black barrel dropped out of the bottom of the plane.

Peter watched it coming with a feeling of absolute helplessness. It looked to him as though the bomb was flying horizontally through the air and spinning slowly, but as it came closer and closer it seemed to drop down as though pulled by some magnet in *Slewfoot.*

It was all so slow and lazy, the black thing floating down toward the boat, the tin vanes on the end of it making it turn around and around.

The hard hammering roar of the plane smacked down on them for an instant and was gone.

The bomb struck the water with a bright, white splash and then exploded. The sea rose first in a curious, smooth, rounded hump and then that burst open and dirty-colored water gushed upward, hesitated, then curled and fell back on *Slewfoot.*

"He's coming back!" Stucky yelled. "Get him! Get him!"

Archer dragged himself out of the seat and screamed at Stucky, "Hold your fire!" Then he swung forward and screamed again, "Hold your fire. Get away from those guns! Wave that flag!"

But the plane was shooting again, the muzzle flashes twinkling like little yellow lights along the leading edges, the bullets again walking toward them in bright splashes across the water.

Goldberg and the Preacher held the flag up as high as they could and waved it as the plane roared toward them, the sound of its engines drowning out everything.

And then Peter heard the Bofors cannon crumping away behind him, heard the clang of the empties hitting the deck. He spun around to see Stucky jammed against the gun as it fired and recoiled, fired and recoiled.

The plane swept close over them, Stucky swinging the gun up, and then it turned suddenly straight down and struck the water.

The impact tore the wings off and broke the fuselage in half. For a moment the empennage stood upright in the water and then slowly sank.

No one came out of the plane.

Archer said, "Have Stucky report to the bridge, Mr. Brent."

"It's too late now," Peter said.

"It's never too late to enforce discipline, Mr. Brent."

Peter climbed slowly down off the bridge and walked slowly aft. Perhaps in the last moments that pilot had seen the flag. Thinking back, it seemed to Peter that in the last few yards of his flight his guns had stopped firing. If only Stucky had held his fire they might have been recognized. Recognized and saved.

But then, he thought, perhaps not. The pilot might have kept on, never seeing the flag, until he hit them and killed them all.

Nobody would ever know.

Stucky was sitting down among the empty shell cases, his back against the gun mount. Mitch was standing back by the smoke generator looking down at Stucky with a curious expression.

As Peter approached he knew that all hands were now thinking the same thing, wondering the same thing. If Stucky had not fired the Bofors, what would have happened?

"Stucky," Peter said, and hated having to do it, "the Captain wants to see you. On the bridge."

Stucky must now be realizing what he had done, Peter thought, as he just sat there against the gun mount. Peter looked over at Mitch, who was still staring down at Stucky. "Well, it was good shooting anyway," Peter said. Then he walked around in front of Stucky and said, "Okay, Stucky. On the bridge."

Stucky's face was gone.

5

The hot, blazing sun poured down from an empty sky upon an empty sea. Archer, who knew the ritual for burial at sea, said the words as he stood beside the depth charge racks, his face white and strained.

And then Stucky, wrapped in one of the canvas gun covers, slid away from *Slewfoot* and struck the water and was gone.

"All right, men," Archer said, "return to your duties."

For once, Peter thought, the man had had some compassion in his voice. He watched Archer walk slowly forward and go below.

Mitch picked up one of the Bofors empty shell cases and stood for a moment just holding it and looking at it and then, with sudden violence, he flung it away. Peter watched the bright brass case turning end over end through the air until it struck the water with a bright splash and sank, wobbling down through the blue water.

"If Stucky hadn't shot him down, we'd be on our way home now," Mitch said savagely. "Even an Army pilot would have recognized that flag after a while."

"After he'd blown us out of the water," Peter said. "Come on, Sko, let's see what we can do. Mitch, you keep the deck. Try to find us another plane. A Navy one, if you can."

Below, in the engine room, Skeeter and the Professor were already at work clearing away the last of the wreckage made by the exploding shell. Now, with sunlight pouring down through the hatch, things didn't look so hopeless.

But by nightfall Peter realized how hopeless it actually was. While Sko worked on the engines Peter had gone over the side to look at the propeller shafts and jammed rudders. With Mitch and Jason standing shark guard with carbines, he had dived under the boat to find the rudders hopelessly jammed hard over, one propeller gone, the other two frozen in the outboard strut bearings, the shafts badly twisted.

As the sun went down with an almost startling suddenness, Sko climbed wearily up into his tractor seat. Through the open hatch the now dark sky began to twinkle with faraway stars. Peter started to turn on the lights but thought what's the use and sat down on a toolbox and leaned wearily back against the bulkhead.

"The only chance we've got," Sko said in the darkness, "is to pull one of the engines and get some new bearings in it. For that we need an A-frame built up on deck. We haven't got an A-frame or anything to make one out of."

"Even if we got an engine running," Skeeter said from his darkness, "what could we turn with it?"

"Pull the best shaft," Sko said, "straighten it and put it back. For that we need shallow water so a man can stand up and work on it. What have we got here, Peter?"

"About a thousand fathoms," Peter said, not caring much, for anything over one fathom was too deep.

The Professor went over and turned on the lights. "This is what is known as an academic and footless conversation," he told them as he got out a notebook and studied it. "You said we were drifting north about a hundred miles a day, didn't you, Peter? Okay, *if* we could build an A-frame and *if* we could pull an engine and *if* we could fix the props and rudders in this deep water: it would take *at least* four or five days to do all those things. I figure longer. So what good would it do? We've got enough gas to run"—he looked at his notebook—"three hundred and ten miles on one engine at dead slow. Say we had drifted five hundred miles by the time we could get her under way. We run back three hundred and where are we? Right where we are now—nowhere."

Peter looked past the dim light and up at the stars in the now black sky.

"Any chance of getting some chow out of the Captain?" Skeeter asked him. "That little snack we had at noon isn't holding me."

"I'll see," Peter said, "but I doubt it."

As he went forward, he stopped in his cabin and got the sextant and chronometer, wondering as he did so why he was doing it. What difference did it make where *Slewfoot* was on this limitless ocean.

He went on into the dayroom to find Goldberg feeding Britches some water.

"It's pretty salty," Britches said.

"It's the best we've got," Goldberg told him. "Next time it rains we'll get some good water."

"How you feeling, Britches?" Peter asked.

"Fine," the boy said, "Just fine."

"Don't hurt?"

"Not much, but I sure could use some fresh water."

"There isn't any," Peter said. "But it'll rain pretty soon. It always does."

"I never thought I'd be praying for rain," Britches said.

"Keep it up," Peter said and climbed up on deck. No one was forward, or amidships, or aft. Peter climbed on up to the bridge to find Mitch sound asleep in the canvas chair, his feet up on the tank compartment. Peter woke him up by sliding his feet off so that they flapped down on the deck.

"You supposed to be on watch?" Peter asked.

"Not me," Mitch said. "Nobody told me I was on watch."

"Who is then?"

"Jason or somebody, I guess."

Peter handed Mitch the chronometer. "Are you awake enough to read this thing?"

Mitch looked at the chronometer. "Ten-twenty."

"I want it down to split seconds, Mitch."

"What's up, skipper?"

"I'm not the skipper. Go in the chart house and when I holler 'Mark' write down the time. It's got to be exact, Mitch."

"Exact it will be," Mitch said, getting out of the chair.

Peter hadn't taken a star sight since his days in the school in Rhode Island, and now he found that taking a sight from the moving bridge of a small boat adrift in a restless sea was a lot different from standing on dry land with a professor at your elbow.

He braced himself in the bridge with his knees and elbows and held the sextant up with both hands. For a long time he could not hold a star in the little mirror long enough to bring it down to the horizon, but after a while he caught on. "Mark!" he called out to Mitch in the chart house. Mitch called the time back and Peter read him the angle.

He shot three of the brightest stars he could find and then went into the chart house to work out the sight. It took him more than an hour, but at last he had a tiny triangle penciled in on the chart of the Bismarck Sea. He pointed to it with pride and told Mitch, "That's exactly where we are, Mitch, me boy. Right there." Then he got the dividers and measured off the distance between the star fix and the last dead-reckoning position. "We've moved a hundred and fifty-seven miles since we got hit," he said. "I guess the storm really shoved us for a while."

He got the parallel rulers and laid them across the two positions and then walked the rulers up the chart on the same course, lightly penciling in the line.

The islands of the Bismarck Archipelago form a long, rather narrow horseshoe lying on its side with its open end pointing toward the west. New Guinea forms the southern curve of it, New Britain and its string of westerly islands the northern. At the extreme tip of the northern islands are the Admiraltys.

The penciled line of the course *Slewfoot* was being moved along passed by the last little group of the Admiralty Islands.

Passed them. To the west.

Peter got the dividers and measured over from the penciled line to the dots of the islands.

Twenty-two miles.

"Twenty-two miles," Peter said to himself.

"To where?" Mitch asked.

"See those islands? We're going right by them."

Mitch leaned over the chart studying the islands. "Who lives on 'em."

"Natives," Peter said. "Like the ones in New Guinea."

"With those red gums?"

"I guess so."

"Any Japs?"

"I don't know. Probably some—a few, anyway."

"Mr. Brent," Archer's cold voice said from behind them.

Peter turned to see Archer standing in the doorway, one hand gripping the frame.

"I have walked from one end of this deck to the other, Mr. Brent," Archer went on, "and I have not found a single man on watch."

"I think he just went below for a moment," Peter said, hoping that Jason would appear as suddenly as Archer had.

"Then he should have gotten a relief. What sort of ship are you running that in these perilous waters you allow her to be totally unguarded?"

"Well, I'm here," Peter said.

"Do you consider lallygagging in the chart house standing an alert watch, Mr. Brent?"

"I'll get someone up here," Peter told him.

"I think it's time for this crew to realize that discipline is all that will save their lives," Archer said. "From now on, night and day, I want you to see to it that there are five men on watch, *on deck*, at all times." Without waiting for an answer, Archer turned and disappeared in the darkness.

When Peter turned back to the chart he found Mitch looking at him with a curious, hostile expression. "Are you going to let him get away with that?" Mitch asked.

"Go read the book," Peter said, picking up the dividers again. "We're still in the Navy."

Archer's voice suddenly blasted out of the intercom. "Jason, Mitchell, Welborn, Goldberg, and White report immediately to your watch stations."

Mitch was still looking at Peter with that disdainful, questioning expression. "Why should five men have to stand on their feet all night when all it takes is one man?" he asked quietly. "Why don't you go tell Archer to get with it?"

Peter didn't answer as he unpinned the chart, rolled it up and left the chart house.

On his way down the hatch he ran into Jason and the Preacher coming topside. "What's going on?" Jason asked.

"You're on watch," Peter said and went on down to his cabin.

As Jason and the Preacher came out of the hatch, Mitch on the bridge whispered down, "Hey! You guys. Up here." Then he leaned over as Goldberg and the Professor appeared on the foredeck. "Up here! Up here!" he whispered to them.

When they had gathered, Mitch said, still whispering, "Jason, you watch aft, Goldberg, you watch amidships and Professor, you watch forward. If Archer shows, break it up."

"What is this, Mitch?" the Preacher asked.

"This is a mess," Mitch said. He looked at the five men in the dark and went on. "I thought Brent was a man. I thought he was about the only officer who really cared what happened to a crew. Well, I was wrong. He's just like all the rest of the officers—all he's interested in is keeping his thumb on his number, getting himself promoted and nabbing some shiny medals he doesn't deserve."

"Take it easy, Mitch," the Preacher said.

"I've taken it easy with him as long as I'm going to," Mitch said. "You weren't here, Preacher, when Archer told him to post a heel-and-toe watch for all hands. What did he do? Nothing! He just stood there like a little sailor boy and let that maniac get away with it." Mitch stopped and looked at them again. "I thought all we had against us was Archer, but now I know he's against us too. What are we going to do about it?"

"What *can* we do?" the Preacher asked. "What good will mutiny . . ."

Mitch cut him off. "Don't preach to me, Preacher. This won't be mutiny. This'll just be saving our lives. Don't you see what's going on? Archer and Brent are going to eat all the chow—they're going to stay alive while we drift around until we die. So here's what we do—there're ten of us, not counting Britches, and two of them. Now I just saw Brent chart the course we're on, and we're going within twenty miles of some islands. When we get there—maybe tomorrow night or the next—we'll get what chow they haven't already eaten, then we'll take the raft and row over to those islands. Man, we'll be like in paradise. Plenty of food, plenty of those dusky maidens, plenty of everything . . ."

The Preacher said quietly, "Aren't enough people getting hurt without this sort of thing, Mitch?"

"Who said we'd hurt 'em? If they want to ride the boat, let 'em ride it. We'll just tell 'em we're leaving and if they don't try to stop us nobody gets hurt."

"It makes more sense than drifting around until we starve to death," Jason agreed. "Two thousand miles . . . we'll all be dead."

"Except them," Mitch said. "They've got the food."

"They'll share it," the Preacher said.

"In a pig's eye they will!"

"Even if they did," Jason said, "it won't be enough for thirteen people. Do you realize how long we might drift, Preacher? *Weeks! Months!*"

"I think the only guy we'll have trouble with is Sko," Mitch said. "He still thinks Brent's the fair-haired boy."

From the darkness Goldberg said quietly, "Sko and me, Mitch."

"What are you, Goldberg, chicken or something?" Mitch whispered angrily. "This boat is never going to reach the Philippine Islands, and even if it did, so what? The Philippines are *crawling* with Japanese. Archer and Brent wouldn't live ten minutes after they hit the beach. Neither would we if we went along with 'em."

"I'm going where Brent goes," Goldberg said.

"Listen, Gerry," Mitch said, calmer now and persuasive. "Brent was a good guy. I admit that. When he was Exec under Jonesy he was a good guy, and even when he was skipper he was a good guy. But this Archer has beaten him down to nothing at all. He isn't like he used to be."

"You can say that again," Jason agreed.

"He's the same," Goldberg said.

"All right!" Mitch said angrily. "You and Sko stay and drift around until you die. . . . Okay, what about the rest of you?"

"Sounds good to me," Jason said.

"If there's no violence, Mitch. . . . Nobody gets hurt. . . ." the Preacher said.

"I know Murph and Sam'll go. So will Skeeter and Willie. What do *you* say, Professor?"

"I say let's look at the character of Peter Brent," the Professor said in that way of his. "When we were fooling around with those transports I think you said he was a coward, didn't you, Mitch?"

"Well, at first . . ."

"That's what I mean," the Professor said. "At first he looked like a coward, but when he got going he went pretty well, didn't he?"

"That was before Archer," Mitch argued.

"Archer hasn't changed his basic character," the Professor said. "So I'm going to give Brent time to get going."

"How much time?" Mitch demanded. "A week? In a week we'll be in the Pacific. Just as good as dead."

"I'll give him until the rest of you are in the raft," the Professor said. "Then . . . I'll get in too."

"Good," Mitch said. "Now, Goldberg, you and Sko are the only ones who can mess this up by telling either Archer or Brent. So what are you going to do? Squeal on your shipmates?"

Goldberg took a long time to answer, but finally he said, "No."

"I don't think Sko will, either. So we're set," Mitch declared. "Now every time Brent takes a star sight I'm going to be there. I'll watch what he marks on the chart and when it's time to go I'll pass the word. We've got to do it fast and do it right. But until the last minute, we've got to be good little sailors, no matter what Archer or Brent make us do. Right?"

They were about to answer when Brent's voice came flatly out of the intercom. "Bridge?"

Mitch leaned to the intercom. "Bridge, aye aye."

"Mitch? Listen, break out the life raft and check it over real good. Then bind a one-inch line around the gunwales with a good-sized eye in it astern. Okay?"

For a moment Mitch stood staring at the intercom and then he said, "Yes, sir."

In the darkness Goldberg laughed quietly. "Well, Mitch, ol' buddy," he said, "it looks like those stupid officers have beaten you to the punch."

6

Peter Brent sat in the little cabin—hardly more than a closet—with the charts and books spread out on the fold-down desk and the bunk.

"Vailulu Madness," he read, "is a growing cult among the Melanesians of the Bismarck Archipelago. Sometimes known as Cargo Cult from the pidgin English of these people— cargo being in pidgin a man's possessions—it is basically a movement to get rid of all aliens, taking their 'cargo' in the process. Since these tribal natives are only two generations removed from the Stone Age this Vailulu Madness takes forms of extreme violence, including death by torture, murder of women and children and, in some cases, cannibalism. The cult seems to have originated in the Admiralty Islands, spreading from there to the more populated areas of the Archipelago.

"The inhabitants of the Admiralty Islands are a primitive, tribe-oriented group still clinging to many Stone Age practices. All adults and many children chew the narcotic plant, betel, which accounts for the characteristic bright red color of their gums. Adults also file their teeth to points. They are adept at sailing the outrigger canoes, making voyages of many hundreds of miles, but have few modern skills."

And then, underlined in the book, was the last sentence: "*Anyone coming in contact with the natives of the Admiraltys should regard them as extremely hostile, dangerous and treacherous with allegiance to no one.*"

Peter closed the book slowly and stared at the chart with the penciled line of *Slewfoot's* course.

The Admiralty Islands lay ahead and to the starboard of the course. Peter had seen natives in New Guinea—almost naked, fuzzy-haired dark people, red-gummed and teeth filed to points—and he had not been attracted to them. There was no friendliness in their eyes, no appreciation for the many things the men had done for them.

Peter remembered particularly their worship of the crocodile. He had seen many carvings by these people of crocodiles, all of them in the process of eating people. The carved people were always half devoured, feet first, the rest of their bodies half out of the critters' mouths. And every one of the people had this silly smile on his face as though it was an honor to be swallowed by a crocodile.

Peter sat with the words of the book still strong in his mind—hostile, dangerous, treacherous . . . cannibalism, slow torture, murder—and, equally strong, the thought of the terrible wastes of the Pacific Ocean with the great storms roaring across it, or the mind-destroying calms. And he suddenly thought of what a destroyer captain had once told him—of a wave so enormous that it rolled the destroyer more than 90° and towered above the ship like a mountain of water. How could *Slewfoot* survive a sea like that?

Peter wished that Jonesy were here now to help him, to talk with him and, together, decide what to do. For there was little time left and the decision had to be made. The simple decision: try to get the boat over to the Admiraltys, or let *Slewfoot* go on out into the Pacific and take her chances across the limitless distances and the great hazards of that ocean.

But he knew that he would have to decide this thing alone— Archer would not help him.

And if he decided to try to beach the boat in the Admiraltys, Peter was sure that Archer would be dead set against it.

Added to all the rest of his troubles, Peter thought of the crew. That a mutiny was in the making he was sure, with Mitch as the ringleader. Peter doubted if all of the crew were behind Mitch in the thing—Sko and Goldberg would be the last to join him—but it was only a question of time, and if Mitch were given the time it would take to drift for two thousand miles, mutiny was inevitable. That he, Peter, would go down with Archer was a fact.

It *had* to be the Admiraltys. Somehow they *must* reach those islands. His life—and the lives of the crew—hung on getting to land *soon*. It would probably mean trouble with the natives, but *Slewfoot* was still armed and dangerous. Peter was sure she was as dangerous as any Stone Age savages.

He rolled up the chart, got the tide tables and the books and went across the passageway to Archer's cabin.

Mitch, in the dayroom, saw him cross the passageway and whispered to Jason, "There he goes to eat our chow."

Goldberg, who had been sitting beside Britches, got up in the dark and crossed over to Mitch. "I've been thinking," he said quietly, "and I don't like it, Mitch. I want you to knock off this talk. I don't care what you and the rest of the guys do, just knock off the talk."

"Can you make me, Goldberg?"

"Let me ask you one thing. Has Peter Brent ever put you down for foul-ups you've made on this boat? The answer is No. So you stop putting him down."

"Can you make me, Goldberg?"

Goldberg stood over him in the dark and said, very quietly, "I can make you, Mitch." Then he turned and went back to Britches.

"Let's get out of here," Mitch said to Jason.

Goldberg watched them go, pausing outside the captain's cabin, trying to hear what Brent and Archer were talking about.

"What's up with Mitch?" Britches asked.

"He's yakking about mutiny."

"Maybe he's right. Archer . . ."

"You knock it off too," Goldberg said. "Any mutiny on this boat will be against Peter too, because he's an officer and he'll behave like one. And if Mitch tries it, Peter will go against him. He'll go until one or the other gets it."

"For *Archer?*" Britches asked, surprised.

"Not for Archer. Not for us. For the boat. He's not going to let a mutiny happen on *Slewfoot* if he can help it."

"No, I guess he wouldn't."

In Archer's cabin Peter spread the chart out on the bunk and got the books and tables ready. Archer sat at the desk reading. He had not spoken to Peter since telling him to come in.

Now Peter was ready. "Adrian," he said.

Archer put his book down slowly and turned. "Yes?"

"You're senior to me, and you're my commanding officer, but I'd appreciate if it you'd forget that for a little while so we can talk. We're in trouble. More trouble than just being adrift and if we don't do something about it—together—we're going to have a mutiny on our hands."

Archer turned back to the desk. "Mr. Brent, have you ever heard of a man named William Bligh?"

"Is he in the boats?"

"He was in a boat once. It was an open boat, only twenty-three feet long. In it with him were eighteen men and they lived for forty-two days and three thousand six hundred miles across the open sea."

"Oh, you're talking about the *Mutiny on the Bounty* man, Captain Bligh."

"Captain Bligh. And do you know how he managed to keep those eighteen men and himself alive across all those miles? *Discipline,* Mr. Brent." Archer picked up the book he had been reading. "Read the account of that voyage sometime. It will do you a lot of good."

"That happened two hundred years ago. I'm talking about now!"

"Bligh was a master seaman and a great commanding officer who rose to the rank of vice admiral because he would not break his rule of discipline, discipline for himself and for the men serving in his commands."

Peter stared at this man as, slowly, he began to realize at last what made Archer run. Bligh. William Bligh, vice admiral in the British Navy. A man whose name survives in history because men under him mutinied not once, but twice, against his harsh discipline. Archer, Peter thought, must be a man without a character of his own, or at least a man who could not bring his character with him into the Navy.

"Do you think, Adrian, that you're going to be another Captain Bligh?" Peter asked quietly.

"I'm going to base the command of my ship on the principles of discipline—as Bligh did."

Now Archer was becoming clearer, and as Peter now saw him he realized that Archer was far more dangerous than he had first thought.

"You do it any way you want," Peter said. "But right now I want to suggest that we try to get over to the Admiraltys. I think we can."

"The Admiraltys are in the hands of the enemy," Archer said.

"What isn't? What land, what island between here and China isn't in the hands of the enemy?"

"In the Philippines there is a strong guerrilla organization. We'll be safe in the Philippines."

"Then why didn't General MacArthur stay there? Look, Adrian, we've got a chance in the Admiraltys and no chance on the open ocean. Willie says that he might be able to fix the transmitter in a day or so. And in shallow water we can get the engines going again. In the Admiraltys we're only three hundred miles from home, man!"

"We are not taking this boat into the Admiralty Islands, Mr. Brent."

Peter sat down on the bunk. He knew now that the time he had been putting off for so long could not be put off any longer. But what he knew he had to do gave him no pleasure, no sense of accomplishment. It only made him ashamed—and sad.

"Adrian, listen to me. Be Captain Bligh with somebody else. Don't try to take us across the Pacific just to prove a theory. We won't make it, Adrian.

"We *will* make it, Mr. Brent."

Well, here it is, Peter thought. The end of Ensign Brent, Peter, USNR. He could be shot for this. Court-martialed and shot.

"Have you got the ship's log down here, Adrian?"

"Of course."

"Then make this entry in it. As of now I am not taking orders from you and I am going to do everything I can to get this boat to the Admiralty Islands."

Archer looked up at him with, at last, a real expression on his face—surprise and disbelief.

"So—you are the mutiny."

"Call it that," Peter said.

"Before I make that entry I'm going to read you the Navy regulations regarding mutiny—in time of war, Mr. Brent. For your own good."

"You don't have to. Just make the entry."

"Very well. I am also going to enter the fact that I have put you under arrest and have confined you to your quarters under armed guard."

"No," Peter said, "you're not going to do that. Some of the men are on the verge of mutiny now, Adrian. If you try to arrest me they will mutiny."

Archer took down the log, opened it and wrote for quite a while. When he finished, he looked up at Peter and said with that same cold voice, "From the moment I took command of this ship I have considered you an incompetent officer, interested only in your own welfare. I have given you a great deal of leeway, Mr. Brent, and now you have proven your incompetence not only as an officer but as a seaman. I happen to *know* that without power it will be impossible to get this boat anywhere near the Admiralty Islands."

Archer pushed himself up out of the chair and faced Peter. "I'm going to give you one more chance, Mr. Brent. I'm willing to forget this entire conversation. At least, I will forget it officially. In return for this I want your co-operation. We have a long and dangerous journey ahead of us."

"Make the entry," Peter said, turning to his chart and books.

Archer laughed and it was the first time Peter had ever heard him laugh. "There's nothing you can do that will change the course of this boat. You'll never see the Admiralty Islands, Mr. Brent."

Peter ignored him and went out. On the companionway going topside with the books and charts he began to shake and there didn't seem to be enough air to breathe. He stopped halfway up the stairs and waited a moment for the shakes to settle. Well, he thought, I did it. End of me.

Goldberg was on the bridge leaning against the windshield. He didn't hear Peter come up and go into the chart house and Peter, suddenly very aware of his new position but not yet sure how to handle it, did not speak as he passed behind Goldberg.

In the chart house he waited a moment before turning on the light. He was very confused now as he was faced with the consequences of what he had done. Only one thing was clear: the crew must not know that he had mutinied against Archer. If they found out, it would make their own plans for mutiny justifiable. He wondered, as he flipped on the light, if Archer could come out of his dream world far enough to realize that also.

Peter pinned the chart back to the table and advanced the star fix up the line the two hours since he had shot it. Then, with the rulers, he laid a course to the Admiraltys, laying it well eastward of the islands to compensate for the westerly force of wind and current.

Going out on the bridge he found Goldberg still leaning on the windshield. "Evening, Gerry," Peter said.

"Evening, Peter."

"Quiet night."

"Yeah. Real quiet."

In his mind, Peter was breaking the crew in half, and as he did it he was weighing the key men, balancing them against each other. Mitch was the heaviest and most dangerous of them all—to counterbalance Mitch was the first problem. The next, he guessed, was probably Sam. The weight of Murph would depend . . . if Murph was thrown in with Mitch he would weigh a lot. With Sam he would weigh less.

And then there was Sko and Goldberg.

Peter leaned over the rail and called down to Mitch on deck. "Mitch, will you come up here a minute, please."

There was animosity even in the way Mitch walked as he strolled aft. Or, Peter wondered, was he just imagining it?

"Yeah?" Mitch said as he came on the bridge.

"How many paddles have we got, Mitch?" Peter asked him.

"Paddles?" Mitch asked, his voice now undoubtedly surly and suspicious. "What do you want with paddles?"

Peter looked at him in the starlight—and remembered the old Mitch. Always griping about something, always threatening to put in for a transfer, always saying he'd get out of the boats and never put foot on one again—but always a formidable man in a fight. And a man who had once had two hands for *Slewfoot* when she needed them. A man you could count on, always.

"To paddle," Peter said quietly.

"Paddle where?"

"How many, Mitch?"

"There're four in the balsa raft and two in the rubber boat."

"Fine. Break 'em out and break out that new line we liberated in Milne."

For a long time Mitch made no move to obey him and didn't answer. Finally he said, "What for?"

Goldberg, who had been listening, now walked across the bridge and stood, looming over Mitch.

Peter knew then that he could wait and Goldberg would handle this situation for him, but he didn't want that. He was saving Goldberg for greater emergencies than this.

Peter said quietly, "Because I say so, Mitch. Okay?"

"You say so," Mitch said and left the bridge.

"Peter . . ." Goldberg said.

"In a minute," Peter told him, going aft to the open engine room hatch. "Sko," he called down, "can you spare Skeeter for a while?"

Then he went over to the radar shack where Willie was sitting staring at a schematic with a baffled expression. "Willie, you need a little fresh air."

Peter turned back to Goldberg. "Go get the Preacher out of the sack and on deck."

"He's on the next section of the watch, Peter. Maybe he ought to sleep."

"The skipper and I've got a new deal," Peter said.

He went with Goldberg down to the foredeck where Mitch had the paddles and coil of line.

Peter waited in silence, with Mitch silent beside him, as the men came forward, one by one.

This is the way he would divide them, Peter decided. Against the strength of Mitch he would pit the strength of Goldberg, the weakness of Willie and Skeeter, and the goodness of the Preacher. Against the lesser strength of Sam and Jason, and the unknown quantity of Murph, he would throw the quiet power of Sko and the intelligence of the Professor.

And these two halves would not be allowed to get together. There would be no more of Mitch intimidating and persuading the others in the darkness of the dayroom or the remoteness of the depth charge racks. No more of Mitch and Sam and Jason and Murph pooling their strength and gaining more from each other.

"Okay," Peter said to the five men gathered on the foredeck. "Secure that line to the forward bitt and the other end to the sling on the raft. Skeeter, get the boarding ladder."

The raft was a clumsy oval thing of balsa, seven feet long, three wide and meant only for survival, but it was all he had and it would have to do.

When all was ready—the rope secured to the raft and the boat, the ladder dangling over the side—Peter looked at the five men. "Let's go," he said. "Drop the raft and get in."

He could feel them staring at him, feel their animosity. He waited, knowing that it would be Mitch.

"We get in," Mitch said, "and then you cut us adrift. Is that the idea . . . sir?"

"If you want to live, get in that raft," Peter said.

7

*It was bru-*tal punishment. For the first hour they paddled without too much trouble, Goldberg, Mitch and Willie on one side, Peter, the Preacher and Skeeter on the other. By the second hour their hands were beginning to hurt and their bodies, jammed together in the raft, were one solid ache.

In the dark it seemed so totally useless, so like a dream of running away as hard as you could but not moving. The water against the paddles just seemed to slide away, the raft and *Slewfoot* remaining motionless under the stars.

At the end of the second hour they changed crews, Mitch and his gang climbing wearily back aboard while Sam, Jason, the Professor, Sko and Murph climbed into the raft. Peter decided to paddle these two hours also just to get the thing settled down, for if he could keep them at it they were going to be paddling this way—two hours in the raft, two hours resting in *Slewfoot*—for a long, long time.

At the end of the second two hours the sun came up and they changed crews again. Peter, exhausted, could hardly pull himself up the rungs of the swaying boarding ladder.

Archer was standing on the foredeck as Peter crawled over the side and lay for a moment, catching his breath.

Archer said, coldly amused, "I've heard of shoveling sand against the sea, but this is the first time I ever saw it done."

Peter got up on his hands and knees and then to his feet. Ignoring Archer he looked out at the raft. Mitch and Goldberg were arguing, but the raft was too far away for him to hear what they were saying. The other three men were just sitting, paddles in their laps, listening. Peter felt utterly defeated as he stood, watching, and no paddle touched the water. But then they began, the paddles dipping in unison.

Peter turned then to Archer. "I want the food, Archer. All of it."

Archer looked at him for a moment and then said, "I've estimated that it will take us twenty-three days to reach the Philippines. I've divided the food into twenty-three portions, one portion to be again divided among all of us, once a day."

"Archer," Peter said, "I've mutinied against you, remember? From now on, I'm running this boat. Don't interfere with me."

"You can run the boat, but I am going to control the food."

"Don't you understand what I just said?" Peter asked him. Then he turned and went down the hatch.

In the dayroom the first crew were already sound asleep, flaked out in exhaustion on the bunks. Only Britches was awake and, to Peter's surprise, up on his feet, his arm in a sling Archer must have made for him.

"Are we getting there?" Britches asked.

Peter shrugged as he went on through the room. Britches followed him. "I'm feeling fine. I could paddle some."

"Maybe later," Peter said, trying the knob of Archer's cabin and finding it locked.

Peter slammed a shoulder against the door, breaking it open and realizing as he did it the mistake he had made with Britches standing there watching. "Lost the key," Peter said lamely as he went into the cabin and began bringing out the food. "What you can do, if you feel like it, is help me get up some chow for these guys. I think we've got about two days to go, but let's play it safe and make it three. Divide everything into three piles. We'll eat one a day.

"Hey, look at the peaches! Something to drink."

"That's an idea," Peter admitted, suddenly feeling his own thirst. "We'd better take it real easy on them in case it doesn't rain."

When it was time to shift crews again, they stopped long enough for all hands to eat, Archer alone refusing any of it.

The food did them a great deal of good, and the brackish water combined with a little of the peach juice slaked the thirst that was now becoming a major problem.

Peter went into the raft for the next four hours, but at the end of them he was done. Goldberg helped him over the side and down the companionway to his cabin, where he fell into his bunk.

He woke up to find the room dark and a strange sound outside, which, for a moment, he couldn't explain.

It was rain, a fine, gentle, windless rain. As he came on deck the first thing he looked for was the raft, and it was out there, Mitch's crew paddling steadily in the rain.

Sko and the others had already rigged up the gun covers

and the rainwater was running beautifully into the tanks.

The rain had one drawback which Peter almost resented. He could not see a star in the sky. Now they had been paddling for more than twenty hours and Peter wanted to know whether or not it was accomplishing anything. Or, he wondered, was it really a dream and the boat was not moving.

He went into the raft with Sko's crew and paddled with them in the rain until it stopped. Then, as the sky cleared, he went aboard and ran for the bridge. In the dark he saw Mitch come out on deck and follow him.

"Want me to write down the time for you?" Mitch asked.

"Fine."

"What can you tell after you get a fix?" Mitch asked.

Peter looked at him, wondering what he really meant by this innocence and this innocent question. "I can tell whether you're pulling your weight in the boat," Peter said, handing him the chronometer.

An hour later, the sights worked out, the little triangle drawn on the chart, Peter could have cried—and would have cried if Mitch had not been standing at his elbow.

After twenty hours of paddling, *Slewfoot* had been pulled only five miles closer to the Admiraltys. And in that same twenty hours she had drifted a hundred and seven miles closer to the wastes of the Pacific.

"Not doing much good, is it?" Mitch asked. "Five lousy miles."

"That's five miles closer than we were last night," Peter said, putting the sextant and chronometer away.

The night was long, but it could not compare to the blazing day that followed. No wind blew to cool them as they sat in harsh discomfort in the raft and paddled, stroke after stroke, their hands raw now, their muscles like strings of fire.

And then it was night again, with the stars shining cool and faraway. Mitch was there again as Peter took his careful shots, catching the brilliant and magnified stars in the little square mirror and delicately bringing them to touch—and only touch—the far, dark horizon of the sea. With infinite care now—for to be right was important—he measured the angles, cautioned Mitch to be accurate to the fraction of a second, checked and rechecked the data from the tables.

In the twenty-four hours of heartbreaking work they had gained ten miles. The span of the dividers looked to Peter like salvation itself, until he put them back on the chart and walked them along the new course they were making.

If his star fixes were right—and he thought they were—*Slewfoot* was now only seventy-five miles away from the Admiraltys. Seventy-five miles south of the islands and twelve miles to the west.

He did the sums in his head slowly, step by step, for he already knew the answer and did not want to reach it again any faster than he had to. Rate of drift: 5 miles an hour. Distance along course of drift: seventy-five miles. Five goes into 75 fifteen times. And fifteen times meant fifteen hours left to paddle. In the twenty-hour period at the beginning, when they were fresh, they had closed the distance by five miles. In twenty-four hours they had closed it—because of the windless day—ten miles. But now the men were dead-tired, with raw and bleeding hands, with only two-hour snatches of sleep for more than forty hours. How could they, Peter asked himself, close those last twelve miles in only fifteen hours? Where could they find the strength and the endurance to do that?

He went down to the foredeck and watched as the raft was pulled back to the boat and the crews exchanged places. Peter followed Sko down the boarding ladder and picked up the extra paddle. "Let's go," he said, his hands so painful that he could hardly force his fingers to bend and grip the handle, now covered with some other man's blood.

Peter paddled with one crew or the other for the rest of the night and then on through the morning. For long periods he just squatted there, his arms moving the paddle in the slowing rhythm, his mind a blank, his body just one long pain.

At noon he got out of the raft and shot the sun, penciling in the line.

He noticed that his hands were dripping blood on the chart as he picked up the dividers and measured again.

The men had done well during the twelve long hours, closing the distance by seven miles.

The current, however, had done better. There were no longer three hours left—only two.

Peter went out on the bridge and looked forward to where the men sat in the raft, slowly paddling. There was no strength left in them as they dipped the paddles and almost let them float aft, then lifted them only high enough to slide them back across the water.

And there, off to starboard, was an island. A green and cool and peaceful island with the palms growing almost down to the sea, their fronds hardly stirring in the gentle, warm wind. An island he could see across only a few miles of water, but they were, each one, a million miles.

Peter stared bitterly at the island and then slowly turned his head and looked northward at the awful majesty of the empty sea.

"Well, Mr. Brent," Archer said behind him.

Peter turned slowly to face him.

"There are your islands," Archer said, "but you'll never reach them. Your mutinous conduct has been all for nothing."

Peter heard someone yelling on deck and looked around. Britches was standing there, yelling and pointing with his good arm.

The men in the raft raised their heads from their chests and looked too. Over the water Peter heard Goldberg cry out, "Land! Land! Paddle! Come on, Mitch, *paddle!*"

The other crew, Sko's crew, came pouring up out of the hatch to stand on the foredeck staring at the island which, already, seemed to be drifting away from them to the south.

Sko suddenly turned and went below. In a moment he was back with a coil of rope. He threw a bowline around the forward bitt and tossed the line into the water. "Come on, you guys, jump in." Then he began pushing them over the side. In a moment they were lined up along the rope, holding it with one hand while they swam toward the island with their free hands and feet. Peter could feel the faint acceleration as their swimming began to pull *Slewfoot's* bow around.

Peter ran into the chart house and took the carbine down from its rack. Running back out he shoved it into Archer's hands. "The least you can do is watch for sharks. Get up there!"

Then he ran down off the bridge.

He was passing the torpedo racks when he suddenly stopped and looked at them.

In the two racks were four torpedoes, 22½ inches in diameter, 13½ feet long, carrying in their noses 600 pounds of TNT. Running free they could make 33½ knots and had a range of six thousand yards with their compressed-air turbines.

He was staring at them as Archer, carrying the rifle, strolled forward, saying, as he passed, "Give up, Mr. Brent. Haven't you punished these men long enough?"

Peter ignored him as he called over to Britches, "Disarm these fish and set them for low speed, depth four feet. Bear a hand!" Then he dived down the hatch and into the chain locker. Hauling out the biggest rope he could find, he dragged it back on deck and ran aft with it to the starboard rack. "Lock the rudders on number one and secure this forward of 'em, Britches."

Then he called out, "Goldberg! Pull her bow around— straight toward the island."

With a bight of the rope, he went forward and secured it to the bitt. Leaning over, he called down to the swimming men, "Haul her around to starboard, Sko. Get her lined up with the island. Then watch out. I'm going to let the fish go."

The men, swimming hard, only looked up at him and swam harder.

Slowly, slowly the bow of *Slewfoot* was pulled by the paddling men and the swimming men around against the current and wind until it was pointing at the island, now less than a mile away.

He ran back to the port rack and helped Britches two-block the line around the rudder of the top fish. "Okay, flip it," he said, helping Britches to roll the rack over and down. "Look out, forward!" he yelled to the swimmers. "Here she comes. Okay, Britches, let her go!"

The torpedo slid out of the rack and fell into the water. For a long moment it just lay there, long, oily and useless, but then the turbine began to turn and the twin counter-balanced propellers began to move and the fish slid away along the side of the boat.

Peter watched the loop of rope straightening out in the water and then snap taut, throwing a shower of sparkling water on the swimmers.

Peter felt the jar as the fast-moving torpedo lunged against the rope. It wasn't much of a jar—just a movement of the boat under his feet—but it was a *movement* and *Slewfoot* began to slide faster through the water.

"Lock the next one," Peter told Britches and then went below and came up with the fire ax. As he went forward with it he saw that Britches already had the picture and was securing the next loop of rope to the last port torpedo.

Archer was standing in the bow, the rifle in his arms, as Peter came forward and stood by the bitt.

"Very clever, Mr. Brent," Archer said.

Peter was counting the torpedo run and had no time for conversation. Now the boat was sliding smoothly, although slowly, toward the island and he did not want to lose the momentum. Figuring the torpedo run at one hundred and ten seconds he decided to fire the second fish after one hundred seconds so that it would be off and running a few seconds before the first one stopped.

"Ninety-nine," he counted, and called down, "Look out, here she comes." Then to Britches, "Fire two!"

The second fish slid out, lay that long moment, then moved ahead. Just as the second loop snapped taut, the first one sagged back into the water. So as not to have the deadweight of the first torpedo acting as an anchor, Peter cut the line and let it drop into the water.

Perhaps he was imagining it, he thought, as he counted off the seconds, but now the boat seemed to be moving faster and faster.

He looked out at the raft and the sight of Mitch and Goldberg and Willie and Skeeter and the Preacher paddling their hearts out made a lump in Peter's throat. These, he thought, are now the men I used to know. The men of *Slewfoot*.

"You guys get out of the way," he called down to the swimmers. "We're going to fire from starboard now."

"She's moving!" Sko called up. "Really moving."

"Ninety-nine! Let her go, Britches!"

Number three slid out and down and was away. Peter cut the rope and counted. Then number four went off, running hot and true and he let it go all the way—a hundred and thirteen seconds—before he cut her loose. He dropped the ax and dived overboard. "We're going to make it," he said, grabbing the rope and beginning to swim. Then, near him, Britches crashed down into the water feet first and paddled with his good arm over to the rope. Without saying anything, he grabbed the rope and began a powerful stroke with his legs.

Peter looked at him and saw that his eyes were squeezed shut against the pain and that the blood was draining fast out of his face while the pain jerked his lips away from his teeth and Peter thought that he was going to cry out, but he swam on, soundlessly.

Then Goldberg's voice floated back to them from the raft. "Okay, you guys, all ashore as is going ashore."

Peter stopped swimming long enough to raise his head and look forward.

The men were out of the raft and wading, waist-deep toward the beach, the rope strung across their shoulders.

"Get back aboard and man the guns," Peter said as he turned loose the rope and dropped back to where Britches, eyes closed, was lying still in the water.

One by one they dragged themselves up the boarding ladder, half carrying Britches with them.

Peter was the last to come aboard and as he got to his feet he found Archer confronting him, the rifle in his hands.

"Well done, Mr. Brent," Archer said. "I was wrong."

"Yes," Peter said. Then he took the gun out of Archer's hands and went forward to watch Mitch's crew walking the rope across the beach and into the palms.

8

Peter was down in the engine room with Sko looking at the total wreck of the center engine when Archer leaned over the open hatch and said, "I think you'd better come on deck, Mr. Brent."

"Okay," Peter said, and turned back to Sko. "What do you think, Sko?"

The badly gnawed cigar drooped dismally. Peter had never seen it at such a dejected angle. "We'll never move this boat, Peter."

There was nothing to do but laugh. "Then we'll set up a little tropical paradise for ourselves and let the war go on without us."

On his way topside he looked in on Willie with the transmitter still in pieces all over the table. "Talk?" he asked.

"No talk. This one"—he waved his hand at the pieces—
"is never going to talk again."

Peter made his way under the roof of palm fronds they had
rigged over the boat as camouflage to where Archer was standing in the stern. "Yeah?" he asked.

Archer pointed seaward.

A small outrigger under sail was sliding past the island
about two hundred yards off the beach. An old man and two
boys were perched on the narrow seats, one of the boys
bailing with a coconut shell. They were wearing only some
sort of bark cloth around their waists, and to Peter it looked
as though their hair was dyed a bright orange.

And then he noticed Jason in the sling of the Bofors, the
long, mean barrel pointing flat-out at the little boat. "Hey,
what are you doing, Jason?" Peter asked.

Jason looked from him to Archer and back but didn't say
anything.

"They haven't seen us," Archer said.

"Hope they don't." Peter kept watching as the boat slid
along smoothly in the bright blue water.

Then one of the boys suddenly stood up in the outrigger
and pointed directly toward them. The other boy and the
man turned to look and then, very fast, they sailed the boat
around and got it on the other tack and started going in the
opposite direction.

"You'd better stop them," Archer said.

Peter turned and stared at him. "Stop them?" he asked.

"If you don't, we'll have a tribe of those savages swarming
over us."

"I can't shoot kids, Archer," Peter told him. "Jason, secure
that gun."

Archer looked at him with a curious, remote expression
and then turned away, saying, "I think you're going to regret this, Mr. Brent."

Peter stayed on the stern and watched the outrigger until
it sailed out of sight around the island. And as he watched

he remembered the words in the book—dangerous, cannibalism, treacherous—all of them.

Why was it, he wondered, that a year or so ago he was a college boy, and now he was a mutinous naval officer forced to decide whether to shoot, in cold blood, a man and a couple of kids he had never seen in his life in order to protect the lives of a dozen men in this strange part of the world.

Perhaps Archer is right, he thought. I'll regret not having shot them. And he knew that he would have shot them if they had been directly threatening *Slewfoot* and her men. But not like this. Not in cold blood.

He went past the chart house, got the carbine and told Willie he was going to take a little look around. He got the binoculars from the bridge and climbed down off the beached boat.

Goldberg and Mitch were out on the beach barbecuing a pig Goldberg had trapped. "Bring back an apple and we'll stuff it in this critter's mouth," Goldberg told him as he went by.

Beyond the deep fringe of coconut palms there was thicker jungle covering a low rise in the ground. Peter made his way through the dim, wet greenness to the highest point. After climbing up on a rock from where he could see over the low underbrush, he got out the binoculars and began to examine the long coastline.

In every little lagoon were the huts of the natives, perched above the water on long poles. Around each hut were canoes and outriggers of all sizes, some of them being paddled, others out in the large bay being used for fishing.

The outrigger he had seen was now sailing fast toward the far shore. He could see the excited wavings of the man and the boys in it, and soon a stream of half naked, dark people came running down to the beach as the boat reached it.

Peter put the binoculars back in the case and climbed down off the rock. In his mind, as he made his way back through the jungle, he was planning the defense of *Slewfoot*, for he was sure that sooner or later the savages would attack her.

They would have to stop everything they were doing on the boat and get out into the jungle and cut away a clear field of fire so that any attack would have to come out in the open. The Bofors could take care of anything coming from seaward, which left the 20-millimeters and .50s and .30s for an attack from land.

They would have to get all the food and coconuts they could gather, too, for it might be a long siege.

But as he hurried toward *Slewfoot*, Peter felt the bitterness of eventual defeat. When the last round of ammunition had been fired, what defense would they have against those hordes of natives he had seen in the lagoons all along the coast?

Goldberg and Mitch had cut up their barbecued pig and were wrapping it in banana leaves when Peter came out of the grove. "I think we're going to have a visit from the friendly natives," he told them. "Except they're not friendly. Mitch, get all hands and clear a field of fire around the boat. Make it as deep as you can."

"That's the trouble with paradise," Goldberg said, "the natives."

Peter ran across the beach to the boat. As he climbed aboard he saw Archer sitting on deck in the canvas chair. "I think they're coming," Peter told him.

"I'm sure they are."

"Okay, so I didn't kill a couple of kids and an old man," Peter said, going below to find Jason.

"Get all the ammo on deck and ready to go," he told him, going on to the engine room.

"Drain the gas, Sko. We're going to have trouble with the natives, and the easiest way for them to get us is to burn us out."

Peter yanked himself up the ladder to the radar shack. "Any chance of making *any* noise with that thing, Willie?"

"None."

"Okay, go help Mitch, will you?" Then, as Willie started

down the ladder, Peter called after him. "Hey, Willie, tell all hands to come back to the boat and get carbines. And tell 'em to keep 'em close-by all the time."

Willie nodded and went on down the ladder.

Peter went forward to Archer comfortably sprawled in the chair. He was surprised to see Archer studying the ship's log.

"The book says these people are pretty mean," Peter told him.

"I read that too," Archer said. "You can only hold them off for a little while. You know that, don't you?"

"Maybe," Peter said. "Depends on what they're shooting."

"Also there are the Japanese," Archer reminded him, taking a little gold penknife out of his pocket. He opened the log, flipped through the pages, stopped, and then very carefully began to cut a page out of the book.

"You're not supposed to do that," Peter reminded him.

"I know." Archer finished cutting the page and handed it to him. "Now there is no record of your mutinous conduct, Mr. Brent."

Peter took the page and glanced at the handwriting. Then he laughed. "You think of some pretty funny things at funny times."

"I know." Then Archer looked at him and Peter was surprised to see how weary and drawn he looked. "I don't think they will attack you before morning," Archer said. "They'll take all night to get themselves worked up to it, and then they'll come."

"I think so," Peter agreed.

"So you've got one more night."

"There's not much I can do with it. We can't even get the boat off the beach now."

Archer slumped down in the chair. "I wanted to be a doctor," he said, almost as though talking to himself. "My father and my grandfather were doctors." He suddenly looked at Peter. "I wanted to save lives, Peter, not take them. I'm in the wrong place, and I don't know what to do."

Peter looked down at him, wondering if at last he was beginning to understand Archer.

"I thought they knew what they were talking about in that school in Rhode Island," Archer went on, "and that if you knew the book of regulations you could command a ship. I was wrong, wasn't I?"

"You didn't give yourself a chance," Peter said. "You'd better get a gun, Adrian." Peter went to the rail and jumped down into the shallow water. As he ran toward the men working in the jungle he looked back and saw Archer still sprawled in the chair.

By nightfall they had cleared a fairly deep area around the boat and had cleared away the camouflage so that the guns could swing in covering arcs in any direction from which an attack could come.

The men trooped back to the boat, each carrying as many coconuts as he could, and as soon as all were on board, Peter set a watch, with instructions to shoot anything that moved.

In the galley, Britches was making chow when Peter came down. "We'd better save that, Britches," he told him. "This may take a long time."

He went on to Archer's cabin and knocked on the door. "Archer," he called and when there was no answer, "*Archer!*"

Peter opened the door. The cabin light was out so he turned it on. Archer wasn't there.

Peter went on to the engine room, which was dark and empty and smelled heavily of gasoline.

On deck he asked the watch if they'd seen Archer and they had not.

It didn't take him long to find that Archer was not on board, and then to find that Archer had taken Jonesy's libberated .38 as well as one of the carbines and six clips of ammo.

What a way to do things, Peter thought. And then hoped that his searching for Archer hadn't been noticed by the crew. They had enough to worry about without that.

Murph went forward through the dark to where Mitch, at

one of the twin .30s, was peering at the dark line of jungle. "Hey, you know something?" Murph whispered. "The skipper's run away. Taken a couple of guns and deserted."

"*Brent?*" Mitch said, surprised.

"*No*, the skipper."

"Yeah? Well, I'm not surprised. That guy never was *with* us. And most of the time he was against us. So let him see how he makes out by himself."

"He could hide someplace and when it's all over he can come sneaking back."

"To what?" Mitch asked. "Murph, there're *thousands* of those cannibals. Thousands. And they get hopped-up on that betel juice and *don't care*. Man, they just keep coming. I talked to the Marines about 'em. You shoot one down and another one just steps over him and keeps on coming. You better save your last round for yourself, buddy."

Murph didn't like the idea of it at all. "Peter says he thinks we can beat 'em back."

"Just trying to make us feel good."

"I wish I'd thought of it," Murph said.

"Thought of what?"

"Like Archer. Take a gun and run. He can hide in a tree or something until it's all over and then he can live here until the war's over or something. They wouldn't find him because they wouldn't be looking for him. I tell you what, Mitch, I think I'll go see if I can find Archer."

"Listen, you cockeyed little Irishman, you get off this boat and I'll do what Peter Brent said."

"What'd he say?"

"He said to shoot anything that moves on shore."

Murph laughed, a little nervously, "I was just kidding, Mitch. You wouldn't shoot *me*, would you?"

"I'd enjoy it," Mitch told him.

"Maybe they'll find Archer anyway and stew him up in a big pot and eat him."

"He's not fit to eat," Mitch decided.

In the dayroom Peter and Britches were getting things ready. As Britches spread a clean sheet over the mess table, Peter got the first-aid kit out of Archer's cabin and started taking the things out of it, lining them up in the galley— bandages in a line, then the sulfa powder, then the kit with the scalpels and needles. "If anybody gets hit I don't know what we can do for him," Peter decided, looking at the bright, sharp scalpels.

"Where's Archer?" Britches asked.

"Asleep."

"Really? I heard he'd deserted."

"No, he's asleep," Peter said.

Britches just looked at him and went on getting things ready.

Peter was looking for the morphine Syrettes. These he knew he could use and had seen how much pain they could stop when a man was hurt.

They weren't there. Nowhere. He went into Archer's cabin and searched it completely. The Syrettes weren't there. Coming back to the dayroom he asked Britches, "Did Archer give you any more of those morphine shots?"

"Naw. I asked him once but he said he didn't want to make a dope addict out of me."

In his mind Peter went from man to man, wondering who had stolen the Syrettes. He couldn't imagine any man on board wanting to use the drugs; couldn't remember any man at any time behaving the way addicts do.

Unless, he suddenly thought, it was Archer.

Now he remembered so many times when Archer had had that vacant look, the times he had moved so wearily and yet had done nothing to make him tired, the hours Archer had spent asleep in his cabin.

In silence, Peter finished with the first-aid kit and went topside.

The moon was up, almost full, in a clear and starlit sky and, for once, Peter welcomed it. On that white, moonlit beach nothing could move toward *Slewfoot* without being seen, and no fleet of outriggers could approach her across the bright sea. For a little while longer they were safe.

"You'd better break it up into watch sections," he told Goldberg. "Half of you sleep and the other half stay on deck."

"You'd better get some sleep yourself, Peter, you look like you'd been pulled through a little hole."

"I guess so."

"Has Archer deserted?" Goldberg asked quietly.

Peter looked at him, remembering what Britches had said about it. "What makes you think so?"

"He's not on board."

"How do you know?"

"*Slewfoot's* not that big."

"Well, I don't think it makes much difference," Peter told him.

"We could use another man on a gun."

"We can take 'em, Gerry," Peter said. "The thing is to get one with every shot. Don't spray it around the way the Army does."

He went below then and stretched out on his bunk. He had not realized how beat he was until he put his head down. Then he wondered if he had strength enough to get up again.

It seemed to Peter that he had not been in the rack five minutes when Goldberg woke him up. "They're coming, Peter," Goldberg said.

Peter lay there, suddenly not caring. Now, at last, he felt weak and defeated with nothing more to call on. Let them come, he thought, come and get it over with. He had fought too long and could fight no longer.

9

Peter lay

there, looking up at the hulk of Goldberg.

And then Goldberg said, "We can take 'em, Peter."

Peter got his feet down on the deck, pushed himself up out of the bunk and with his ruined hands pulled himself up the ladder to the deck. He walked aft with Goldberg to find Murph and Jason on the stern. Murph had his glasses and was studying a long outrigger sailing across the moonlit sea. When he saw Peter, he handed over the glasses.

It was the longest outrigger he had ever seen—the main hull was a single hollowed-out log at least thirty feet long. A much-patched lateen-rigged sail drove the boat smoothly on a westerly course and not more than two hundred yards off the beach.

Jason slid into the Bofors turret and cranked the gun down until the long barrel was depressed below the horizontal. As Peter lowered the glasses he saw the barrel moving slowly in phase with the movement of the boat. "Hold it," he said. "I can't figure it out."

"Probably a recon deal," Goldberg said. "Just feeling us out. Probably a couple hundred more beyond that point just waiting for some sort of signal."

"Then let's wait. Let 'em think we don't expect 'em and then let them have it all at once."

Murph had borrowed the glasses again. "I guess they're lying down in the boat because I don't see anybody."

"Neither did I," Peter said, borrowing the glasses back. "Wait. There's one guy anyway."

"Somebody's got to sit up and look where he's going," Murph decided. "A boat that long could carry twenty or thirty men, couldn't it, Peter?"

"Be a little crowded."

"Maybe fifty," Murph declared.

Suddenly the sail of the outrigger collapsed. Peter could hear the yard rattling down on the wooden hull. The lone man in the boat hauled the canvas in out of the water and then began to paddle.

"Maybe he's just out here fishing," Peter hoped.

The man turned the boat directly toward *Slewfoot* and kept on paddling.

"Fishing, my eye," Jason said. "I could take 'em out with one round now, Peter."

"No, hold it," Peter said, studying the man in the boat. Then he lowered the glasses and looked at Goldberg and Murph. "It's Archer," he said.

For a moment they all stood there, no one with anything to say. Then Peter realized what Archer had done and whirled to Goldberg. "Get all the food. And the water. And the carbines." Then he looked at the big man. "Can you hand hold a .30, Goldberg?"

"I can try."

"Then unlimber one of those, too."

As Goldberg started running forward, Peter called, "And the flag, Gerry. And the charts and codes."

Then Peter jumped down off the stern and ran through the shallow water toward the narrow bow of the outrigger sliding silently toward him. "Archer, are you all right?"

Archer's voice sounded weak, but there was still a trace of the old commanding tone it it. "Bear a hand! They're right behind me."

Through the moonlight the men came running as Peter pulled the bow toward shore. They dumped in food and water and guns, running back and forth between the outrigger and *Slewfoot*.

Peter was positioning the stuff to balance when Sko came up. "I saved some of the gas, Peter," he said.

For a moment Peter didn't understand and then, when he did, he looked over at *Slewfoot*.

They walked back to the boat together and climbed aboard. Goldberg met them on deck, carrying one of the .30-caliber machine guns in his arms, belts of ammo strung over his shoulders. "That's all," he said.

"Okay," Peter said. "Get all the men in the outrigger and sort of balance 'em—you amidships."

Goldberg went on down the ladder. Sko, who had gone below, came up now with two cans of gasoline. In silence he handed Peter one of them and then walked forward. Peter stood for a moment and then, tipping the can, he walked aft, strewing the gas on everything as he went. When the can was empty he walked back to meet Sko, who was carrying a gas-soaked length of rope. He tied one end to the bridge structure and then climbed off *Slewfoot*, paying out rope as he went.

On the beach Peter and Sko stood for a moment longer, looking at *Slewfoot* in the moonlight. "She was a good boat, Peter."

"The best," Peter said. "So let her go."

Sko got a lighter and lit the rope. The pale flame in the bright moonlight ran swiftly up the rope toward *Slewfoot*.

Such a tiny flame, Peter thought, watching it.

Then there was a loud, sucking noise and *Slewfoot* was suddenly completely ablaze from stem to stern.

They turned and ran down to the outrigger where the men all sat, their faces lit by the flames as they looked back at the boat.

Peter got in beside Archer. Goldberg and Mitch had the only two paddles and Peter did not have to tell them to shove off.

"How do you sail this thing?" he asked Archer.

Someone was already pulling the sail up the short mast.

"Simple," Archer said. "Get her on the starboard tack and keep her there. That's all you can do. If the wind gets any stronger Mitch and Goldberg are heavy enough to hold her down if they get out on the outrigger."

They turned her seaward with the paddles and the wind suddenly caught the long, lateen sail. Peter looked up at it and saw the light of the yellow flames wavering on it as the long, narrow boat began to move, her hull hissing softly through the water.

"Here, you steer her," Archer said, moving down off the

narrow little seat. Peter moved up and took the smooth-handled tiller.

He could not look back at *Slewfoot* burning now as he sat, facing forward, watching the belly of the sail and beginning to get the feel of the rudder in the water.

But the men looked back, watching. No one said anything.

After a while Peter asked, "How close are they?"

"You'll see them in a minute," Archer said.

"Are you all right?" Peter asked, for Archer's voice sounded very weak and he was sitting, slumped over, his head down on the gunwale.

"I'm all right," Archer said.

Then Peter saw the lights. Hundreds—*thousands*—of them. Little flickering spots of light all across the sea.

"Torches," Archer said.

"What can we do?"

"Nothing. But you're ahead of them and they can't sail any faster than you can."

The burning torches sent firelit smoke up past the pulling sails and to Peter it looked like hundreds of sails bearing down on him.

"Take all you can," Archer said, raising his head and looking at the sail. "Turn her into the wind until the sail begins to shake a little and then ease her off."

"This way?" Peter asked.

"That's it. Now ease her just enough to fill the sail."

The boat seemed to go faster that way, the lights no longer gaining on him.

Peter looked forward at the men crouched in the narrow hull, the bilge water sloshing around their hips. They were so silent, so motionless.

"How's it going, you guys?" he asked.

"*Man*," Murph said, "we're really *moving*. Mitch, get off my foot!"

"I thought it was a brick," Mitch said, moving as much as he could.

"They're turning," Goldberg said. "Doesn't it look like they're turning?"

They were, the sails now flapping loosely in the light of the torches. In a moment the lights began fading away.

"Murph, did you bring a compass?" Peter asked.

"I forgot it."

"It doesn't make any difference," Archer said. "You can only go where the wind wants you to go."

"Can we get back to New Guinea?"

"I think so."

Peter looked down at him. "How'd you get this boat?"

Archer laid his head back down on the gunwale. "I had to kill some people," he said.

"Mitch," Murph said, aggrieved, "get *off* my foot!"

"You're not using it," Mitch argued.

"Is there anything to bail with?" Goldberg asked. "My barbecued pig is getting wet."

The Professor found the bailing gourd. He looked at it in the moonlight and began to laugh. "Pass this back to Peter," he said.

The handle on the gourd was a carved crocodile swallowing a naked girl. In the moonlight Peter could see the simple smile on her face as though she was enjoying the whole operation. He laughed and passed it back.

"We must be making eight or nine knots," Peter told Archer.

"Ten. These are the fastest sailing boats in the world."

Peter did some rapid short division. "Hey!" he said, surprised. "Hey, you guys. We'll be home in thirty hours."

"I never thought I'd call that stinking jungle home," Goldberg said, "but when I get there I'm going to sink right down to my knees in the mud and kiss it."

Peter turned and looked back. The island seemed far away now, a darker mass above the moon-silvered sea. *Slewfoot* was now only a low, dim glow against the darkness of the island. He turned forward again. "If they give us a new boat, what will we call her?" he asked the men.

"*Slewfoot.* What else?" Murph demanded.

"*Slewfoot Two,*" Mitch said.

"*Slew*feet," Goldberg said.

It was the first time they had all laughed for a long time, Peter remembered, as he sailed on to the south, the long boat going very well.

The sun came booming up with little warning and, in a moment, the cold night was gone and a fine, clear, hot day began. The cramped men stirred around in the boat, moving in the sunlight. Goldberg unwrapped a chunk of the barbecued pig and waved it around.

"What do you call that horrid thing?" Murph asked.

Goldberg stared at him. "That's a Goldberger, Murphy. And a piece of it will cost you a month's pay."

Peter looked down at Archer, who had curled up on the bottom of the boat and gone to sleep some hours before. He was still asleep, his face gray and loose looking.

One of the morphine Syrettes, empty, lay beside him.

The Preacher was next to Archer and, as he moved around to loosen up, he touched Archer's leg. Then, slowly, he touched it again, putting his palm down on it. Then he looked up at Peter. "Peter," he said. Then he pointed at Archer.

Peter leaned over and shook Archer's shoulder.

Archer rolled over, face up in the boat, his eyes and mouth open.

"He's dead," the Preacher said in a low voice.

Peter knew it but touched him anyway and found no pulse.

"Why?" the Preacher asked.

The other men had noticed now and were looking aft.

"The skipper's dead," Peter told them quietly. "Shall we take him home?"

The men thought it over, looking at Archer lying now so

ruined. The Professor said quietly, "The sea is as good a place to be buried as any, Peter."

"All right," Peter said. "Lash the machine gun to him."

"We may need that," Jason reminded him, then held up a belt of ammunition, "but I don't see how we can use all this."

The Preacher and Peter got the belt wrapped around him and then they lifted him up on the gunwale. The wound in Archer's belly had been sewn back together, but it had not healed and was awful. Peter glanced at it and then away and said, whispering, "He must've gotten hit the night the barge hit us. All this time. . . ." Peter looked over at the Preacher. "Say something real good, Preacher."

The Preacher thought for a moment as all the men in the boat watched him and waited, each one sad now, remembering what they had thought of Archer and done to him.

"Our heavenly Father," the Preacher began, "this is the third man we've had to send You and he was as good as the other two. As good even as Jonesy, only we didn't understand him and we didn't give him a chance. We even planned to mutiny against him. But in spite of what we did to him he gave his life so that we could have this little boat and live. Please, Lord, be good to him. His name is Adrian Archer."

The men looked away as Archer's body, sinking, drifted down the length of the boat and was gone.

10

The long, bright, hot day ended with a brilliant splash of emerald lying on the far horizon as the sun went down. It had been a peaceful and quiet day. To Peter it seemed that all the men had withdrawn into themselves, for they, like him, had a lot to think about and the remembrance made them all a little sad.

But with the coming of night and the day's restoring of their strength and the feeling of going home there was a change in them. Slowly they began to talk quietly among themselves, and then to laugh and finally to begin horsing around. Peter let it go until they threw Murph out of the outrigger and promised him that they would not go back and get him. The little Irishman's wails in the night were most heartrending.

Peter turned the boat into the wind and let it drift while they hauled Murph back aboard. "Don't throw anybody else over the side," Peter ordered. "We may need him for food ourselves."

Toward midnight the wind veered around to the northwest and became strong and gusty. At first Peter didn't know how to handle the boat in what was now a following wind; but as soon as he picked out a star he knew was in the southeast and eased the sail, the boat began to *fly*, staying well ahead of the waves, which were now coming from astern.

"Holy mack-e-rel, Amos!" Mitch said. "If this thing had a couple of torpedoes we could put her in the squadron."

All day Peter had marveled at this frail craft and had grown completely confident that it could go anywhere in the world through any wind or sea. It was just a long hollowed-out log with the outrigger booms lashed to it with some sort of flat vines. The outrigger was a shorter, solid log, carved smooth and also tied to the booms with the vines. The mast was a marvel of engineering, for it stood without stays from a step fairly far aft in the hull and supported the long, slanting top yard of the sail.

At this sizzling speed one man had to bail all the time, for water kept slipping in over the side. Other than that, she was perfectly seaworthy.

At midnight Peter turned the tiller over to the Professor and then carefully he stood up, one foot on the hull, the other on the outrigger boom. "I figure we've come over two hundred miles," he told Murph, "so we ought to be seeing something pretty soon—New Britain or New Guinea."

"What's the matter with California?" Murph asked. "Or even Mexico. I dig that Latin beat, man."

Peter was standing there and later he swore he heard it go by, it was that close. In the dark water the familiar white spout rose, hung up there and fell back, while from off to port the car-*umph* of the gun floated over to them.

The men began scrambling around in the boat, grabbing the carbines. Goldberg hoisted the heavy .30-caliber machine gun up in his lap and worked the bolt while Mitch laid out the belt as well as he could in the crowded space.

Whatever it was fired again, this time coming closer. Peter, standing up like a statue, felt as though it was shooting at him personally and he wanted to duck down into the boat, but he stood a little longer searching the darkness and praying that he would make out the low, long sleek outline of a PT.

And there it was, lit now by the muzzle flash of a Bofors. The shell screamed overhead and crashed into the water.

It took Peter a few seconds and some embarrassment when he realized it, but he had been yelling, "Whoa!" for quite a while. He stopped that and began to yell—his hands cupping his mouth—"Don't shoot. We're Americans."

And then Goldberg's big, booming voice drowned out everything. "*Slewfoot!*" he boomed. "*Slewfoot!*"

"I think they want us to stop," Peter said, when he thought he could be heard. "Take the sail down. And keep on bellowing, Goldberg."

Peter watched as the PT swung toward them and approached, coming ahead dead slow, the engines muffled so that she was silent and dark. Fifty yards away she swung again, broadside on, and now Peter could see the men standing at the guns.

No wonder, he thought, the Japs were terrified of the PTs. It was an awesome sight—a floating arsenal—and every gun on board seemed to be aimed right at him.

A voice on the PT said, very calmly, "If they make a move, blast 'em."

"Mike," Peter yelled. "Mike Myers! It's me."

The voice, still calm, floated back. "I'm *me* so who're you?"

"Peter Brent. You know me. *Slewfoot*."

The PT began to move, slowly swinging toward them again. Then it was looming over them, the machine guns pointing down at them.

"Hello, Peter," Mike said pleasantly. "What are you doing in that contraption?"

"Yachting, what else? Come on, take us aboard."

Mike at last seemed surprised. "Is that the whole crew? Where's your boat? You're not supposed to be out here in a thing like that."

Peter was trying to get a grip on the PT but he wasn't tall enough. "Yak-yak-yak," he said, as the outrigger began sliding away.

Mike said to someone in the dark. "Get the boarding ladder. I guess we're going to have to let these bums get on our nice, clean boat."

They climbed aboard one by one, Goldberg bringing the last of his barbecued pig.

When they were all on board, Mike said, "Okay, guns, sink that bunch of junk."

"No," Peter said. "Tow it home. We'll mount a cannon on it and use it for a PT until we get a real one."